The Book of Shadows

OTHER BOOKS BY THE AUTHOR
Flight to Zanakor

* * * * *

SOON TO BE PUBLISHED
The Vishtar Command
The Phantom Doorway
Ace Diamond
Shanghai Passage
The Curious Journal of Fen Nordean
Shadow Star
The Dragon's Teeth of Balodark
Who Goes There?
Black Star Rising
The Chrononauts
Seat of Evil
The Shadow People

The Book of Shadows

by

Walter F. Edwards

authorHOUSE

AuthorHouse™
1663 Liberty Drive, Suite 200
Bloomington, IN 47403
www.authorhouse.com
Phone: 1-800-839-8640

This book is a work of fiction. People, places, events, and situations are the product of the author's imagination. Any resemblance to actual persons, living or dead, or historical events, is purely coincidental.

© 2007 W.F. EDWARDS. All Rights Reserved.

No part of this book may be reproduced, stored in a retrieval system, or transmitted by any means without the written permission of the author.

First published by AuthorHouse 8/1/2007

ISBN: 978-1-4343-2729-1 (SC)

Printed in the United States of America
Bloomington, Indiana

This book is printed on acid-free paper.

CHAPTER 1

It had been raining in New Orleans for the past three days. Not a hard rain, just a warm, gentle downpour that kept things wet and sultry.

Bret Kenway stood on the dark sidewalk outside the door in a sleazy part of town wondering if he was on a fool's errand. Through the grill on the window next to the door he could see into a small room. It was lit by the soft yellow glow of candles. He looked cautiously around and peered through the rain at the nearly obscure number painted over the door.

This was it, he told himself. This was the address the bartender had given him. He chuckled. Given him? he corrected himself. The bartender hadn't given him anything. He had paid twenty dollars for the address of Mamma Daka. Again he nervously looked around. Maybe, he thought, I should have waited until morning to come. But with his search nearly at an end he couldn't wait. He had to find out tonight.

* * * * *

The sun was shining when Bret drove into town five days ago. It had been a long, tiring trip from New York City but he felt it would be well worth the trouble. His apartment back home offered little inspiration for his new book. But New Orleans, with its garish atmosphere and local color, was just the setting for a story about shadowy places, dark characters, and voodoo.

He spent his first day in town searching for a place to stay. He was looking for a particular place. A place with just the right ambiance where he could turn that germ of an idea lodged in the back of his mind into a novel. But none of the apartments he looked at had the right atmosphere. He couldn't shake the idea that he would, somehow, know when he found the perfect place. And he was determined to search till he found it.

* * * * *

The next day he left the city and explored the back roads. It was nearing sunset when he saw the old mansion. It sat back off the road, across an expanse that he felt was once a manicured lawn, now overgrown with brush. He stopped the car and got out. In the gathering dusk he could make out the ancient antebellum structure with its tall chimneys, fish scale shingles, and outbuildings. A rusty iron gate set in a crumbling stone wall barred the weed-choked driveway leading to the property. On the gatepost a corroded brass plate read "Halfrith Hall." A real estate agent's sign hung on the gate, now nearly unreadable from long exposure to the elements.

Perfect, he thought. That's the place. It must have quite a past. Got to find someone to tell me about it. Bret chuckled to himself. But I doubt the real estate agent would be completely honest about the house's background. He chuckled again. Maybe, if I'm lucky, he thought, it might even be haunted.

* * * * *

The next day Bret started his search for details concerning the mansion just as it began to rain. For three days he wandered the streets and haunted the bars and restaurants before finding someone willing to talk about Halfrith Hall.

Most of the people he approached looked at him with a suspicious air reserved for outsiders and denied knowing of the place. Others suddenly remembered important business elsewhere. But the bartender at the tavern on Bourbon Street seemed to have no aversion to discussing it, for a price. He admitted he was not an authority on the subject, but for twenty dollars was willing to direct Bret to someone who was.

* * * * *

The water ran off the brim of Bret's fedora and down his neck. He shuddered and turned up the collar of his raincoat. Haltingly he reached out and took hold of the chain dangling from the doorjamb. Then, with a shrug of resignation, he pulled it. Inside he heard the tinkling of a bell; then silence. He pulled the chain again. Soon he heard the sound of soft footsteps padding toward him and the door creaked open.

Bret suppressed a grin. Mama Daka was all he had been told to expect, and more. She stood blocking the doorway; her smoldering brown eyes riveted on him. Her stern African features stood out vividly in the harsh light of the flashing neon sign half way down the block. The large gold hoop earrings drew attention to her sagging jowls, and seemed out of place with her short, rotund body. The motley colored scarf she wore on her head clashed violently with the rest of her colorful attire.

Is she for real? he asked himself. Or does she wear that voodoo priestess getup for the tourist trade?

"What you want, mon?" Mama Daka asked in a low, rumbling voice with a clipped Cajun accent. "You in trouble, mon? Someone put evil eye on you?"

"No," Bret replied. "I just wanted to . . ."

"People come to Mama Daka when in trouble or need potion," the woman interrupted. "But you say you no in trouble." Mama Daka looked at Bret for a long moment; then smiled. "You too handsome a mon for wanting love potion," she said. "You tall mon with broad shoulders. Any woman happy to be with you. Why you come to Mama Daka?"

"I wanted to talk about the old mansion called Halfrith Hall."

"You no want know about Halfrith Hall," she said, the inflection in her voice making her words sound like a dire warning.

"Why not?" Bret asked. "I only want to know the history of the place before I rent it for the winter."

"Why you want rent that place, mon? Plenty other nice places in New Orleans."

"If I could come in I'll tell you." Bret looked around. "I'm getting pretty wet standing out here on the sidewalk in the rain."

The woman looked around suspiciously. "O.K., mon," she said. "You come in. We talk."

Bret stepped through the garishly painted doorway into a dimly lit vestibule.

"Give me your coat, mon," she said curtly. "Then you sit and tell Mama Daka all about it."

Bret handed the woman his wet raincoat and hat. She tossed them onto a hook above the umbrella stand and motioned him into the parlor. Inside she swept her hand in the direction of a wicker chair.

"You sit, mon," she said.

Bret settled into the chair as she moved to the other side of the table and sat.

The room was small, and in the flickering candlelight Bret could see its walls lined with shelves of dusty bottles. The floor was covered with a thick carpet and the small round table was draped with a black cloth. In the corner, atop a pile of dusty, dogeared books, sat what appeared to be a human skull.

It can't be real, Bret thought. Probably left over from Halloween decorations.

Mama Daka leaned forward, her eyes narrowing suspiciously. "Now," she said, "what you want from Mama Daka?"

"Maybe I should start from the beginning," Bret suggested. Mama Daka nodded. "I'm a writer," he began. "I'm researching for my next book. It's going to be about voodoo." Bret smiled. "And what better place to learn about voodoo than New Orleans," he said. Mama Daka frowned and grunted. "I drove around town," Bret continued, "looking for a place with atmosphere. I couldn't find any that I liked. So I drove out into the country. Just outside of town I saw an old mansion. The iron gate on the driveway was padlocked. But from the road it looked like the perfect place."

Mama Daka held up her hand. "Perfect place to stay away from," she warned.

Bret shrugged and smiled. "There's a real estate agent's sign on the gate," he continued. "It looks like it's been there a long time, pretty weather-beaten."

"Yes, long time. No one want to live there. Better you stay in town. I tell you about voodoo."

"I know the place must have a history," Bret said, ignoring the invitation. "Maybe I could incorporate it into my novel.

"I asked about the place in several bars and restaurants in town. But nobody wanted to talk about it. Finally a bartender told me that if anyone could tell me about Halfrith Hall it would be you."

Mama Daka leaned closer to Bret. "It bad place," she said. "Long time ago a gentle lady murdered there. Murdered by man witch."

"You mean a voodoo priest?"

Mama Daka shook her head. "No," she said, "no voodoo man. No houngan, Mon from across sea. He evil mon." She held out her palm. "You want know about him?" she asked.

"Yes," Bret said. He reached in his pocket, pulled out a roll of bills, and stripped off two fifties. "Will this buy me the whole story?" he asked.

Mama Daka took the money and stuck it in her blouse. "Halfrith Hall," she began, "built in 1735 by Englishman name Barlow Baker. In that times, most people in New Orleans be Canadian, French soldier, slaves, travelers, and many whore woman."

Bret smiled. "Yes," he said. "They seemed to be among the first residents of every new town."

Mama Daka smiled and nodded. "It said," she went on, "Barlow Baker be second son of English earl. His father sent him away to America. Older brother get everything."

"A remittance man," Bret commented.

Mama Daka frowned. "What that mean?" she asked.

"Never mind. Go on with the story."

Mama Daka grinned. "Mon call place Halfrith Hall because in his language it mean happy home." Her smile faded. "But it no be that for him," she said sadly, "even though Englishman have big plantation, grow much tobacco and indigo."

"Why not?"

"No can sell. French ships no like come to New Orleans. Only thing there for sale be tobacco and indigo. Cargo so heavy no make money."

"The volume didn't match its bulk," Bret suggested.

Mama Daka nodded. "Englishman go other place to try sell indigo and tobacco," she continued. "Leave young wife name Anora here in Halfrith Hall. But before he go he hire mon named Perrin Fortier for to paint her picture. Fortier say he artist, but he evil mon, maybe devil himself." Mama Daka heaved a sigh and fell silent, her eyes closed.

"Well," Bret prompted, "what happened?"

Mama Daka opened her eyes and took a deep breath. "While in house Fortier try make hump hump with Anora woman." She held up her hands in a praying gesture and pushed one palm against the other several times. "You understand?" she asked. Bret nodded. "Well," Mama Daka went on, "Anora woman no want make hump hump.

"Fortier mon put evil spell on her. Take her to bed and make hump hump anyway. When she wake up next morning spell gone. She tell Fortier she go to police. He put powerful evil spell on her. Send her to other place. Dark place where no one find her."

"You mean he killed her and buried the body somewhere on the property?" Bret asked.

Mama Daka shook her head. "No, mon," she said. "You no hear me say, he send her to other place? Place of shadows. Place where no one ever come back from."

"You mean to tell me this Fortier person just made her disappear?" Bret asked incredulously. "How could he do that?"

Mama Daka glared at Bret. "No ask how," she said in a stern voice. "He powerful witch. Can do if he want."

"All right, if you say so," Bret agreed, barely able to suppress a grin.

"When her mon come back no can find wife. He hear woman cry all night, but can no find anyone anywhere in house. Soon he leave, no one know where. Since then many people try live in Halfrith Hall. None stay long."

Bret smiled. "Quite a story," he said. "But if this all happened over two hundred years ago how do you know all the details?"

"Mama Daka from long line of voodoo priestesses. Story passed down from one who live then. I hear from my grandmother."

Bret got to his feet. "All right," he said, "I paid for a story and I got one." He smiled. "And," he went on, "I think I got my money's worth. True or not, it'll make great material for my book."

"Now you know about Halfrith Hall you no try live there do you?" Mama Daka asked with a glimmer of foreboding in her eyes.

"Yes," Bret replied. "It sounds real interesting. I'll look up the real estate agent tomorrow."

* * * * *

When Bret stepped from the doorway onto the sidewalk the rain had stopped. The gaudy, flashing neon lights cast eerie shadows on the puddles in the street.

Bret smiled. Just the kind of claptrap the public eats up, he thought. If this book doesn't make it to the best seller list, it'll be damned close. He turned up the collar of his raincoat and started down the sidewalk. As he passed the window next to the door he saw Mama Daka's shadowy figure in the small room. She was sprinkling powder from a bottle onto the table and scratching at it with the severed foot of a chicken. He stood for a moment watching the eerie sight, barely able to hear the soft mumbling as she intoned an incoherent voodoo chant.

CHAPTER 2

Mr. Landry, of Landry Realty, smiled across the desk at Bret. "Well now, Mr. Kenway," he beamed, "so you're interested in the Halfrith property." Bret nodded. "Well," Landry went on, "even though it's in the parish its near enough to the city where you shouldn't have any problem hooking up utilities. And it's close to the road where you'd have easy truck access." Landry leaned forward. "If I'm not being too nosy," he said in a low, confidential tone, "just what kind of business are you in?"

"I'm a writer," Bret replied.

Landry's smile faded. "A writer," he repeated.

"Yes, I want to rent the place for the summer."

Landry leaned back in his chair and looked at Bret with a puzzled stare.

"You intend to live there?" he asked. Bret nodded. "But Mr. Kenway," Landry continued, "that property is listed for industrial use. I didn't know you were interested in the old house itself. I thought you wanted to develop the land. Maybe for an apartment complex or something of that sort."

Bret shook his head. "No," he said. "I just want to rent it for a few months."

"You really want to live there?" Landry asked.

"Yes. That's the idea."

"But why?"

"Inspiration."

"Inspiration," Landry repeated slowly, trying to grasp the logic of Bret's statement. "What kind of inspiration, young fellow?"

"For my new book. Living there I should be able to really get a feel for the subject I'm going to write about."

"But the house isn't livable at all, don't you see. It's unsafe, not structurally sound. It would take a lot of money to put it back into livable condition.

And the furniture in the place is rotten and falling apart. It was left there by the last tenants. They moved out and never came back to get it. That's been over . . ." Landry cleared his throat hesitantly. "At any rate," he went on, "it'd cost a fortune to replace it. Besides, the place has never been wired for electricity. No running water or plumbing either. I don't think there's even a usable privy on the place."

Bret smiled. "There's plenty of brush around," he said. Landry frowned. "Just kidding," Bret assured him. "There must be a place in New Orleans that rents chemical toilets."

"Well now, I don't know . . ."

"Mr. Landry," Bret cut in, "how long has the place been on the market?"

Landry fidgeted in his chair. "Well, it's been a considerable time, but . . ."

"Wouldn't a little rental income be better than nothing?" Bret asked.

Landry grinned. "Well," he admitted, "I guess you're right there." Then, assuming an attitude of aloofness, he went on. "But," he drawled, "you have to understand. A commercial buyer could walk in here at any time. If the place is rented out to you, how am I going to negotiate with them?"

"Tell you what," Bret said. "I'll take the place on a month to month basis, no lease. That way, if you get a better offer you can have me out in no more than thirty days. Anyone interested in developing the property for commercial purposes should be willing to wait that long." Bret shrugged. "Hell," he said, "it would take that long to do the paperwork."

Landry nodded. "Yes," he agreed, "you got a good point there." He smiled. "But I hadn't ever considered renting the property as a dwelling. What do you think would be a fair price?" he asked.

Bret shrugged. "You're the real estate agent," he said. "You tell me."

Landry leaned back in his chair and stared at the ceiling for a moment, then looked back at Bret.

"What would you say to, oh, say two hundred a month?"

"Done."

* * * * *

With Bret's check in his desk drawer Mr. Landry walked him to the door.

"Now if you need anything, Mr. Kenway," he said, "don't hesitate to let me know, you hear."

"I'll do that." Bret smiled at the receptionist sitting at her desk near the door and left the office.

Closing the door after him, Landry turned to his receptionist. "Well, how about that," he said. "That young fellow just rented the old Halfrith Hall."

"I heard," she said. Then shaking her head she added, "But he won't be there long."

* * * * *

With the chemical toilet in place outside the kitchen door and a good supply of bottled water and candles Bret settled down for his first night in the parlor on the second floor of Halfrith Hall. The musty old couch was lumpy and creaked with age as he leaned back and opened his laptop computer. Bret looked around the large room. The high ceiling and corners were in darkness, unreachable by the light of the flickering candles on the fireplace mantle. He smiled.

"All right," he said to himself, "time to get to work. Maybe I can get a few pages of a first draft done before I hit the sack." He glanced at his sleeping bag in front of the fireplace. Maybe, he thought, I should have put that on one of those old canopy beds upstairs. He shook his head. Naw, he chided himself, no use going overboard on this atmosphere business. He looked around the dreary room and grinned. First a title, he thought. At least a working one. How about "The Voodoo Murder?" He winced and curled his lips. Too corny, he though with mild self rebuke. How about "The Curse of Halfrith Hall?" Or, maybe even better, "The Secret of Halfrith Hall." Bret took his fingers off the keyboard and gazed into the shadows. No, he thought, that sounds too much like a romance novel. Got to have at least a hint of voodoo. He looked back at the blank screen on his computer. Or maybe not, he thought. That could be a surprise to the reader. Then slowly, with no conscious effort on his part, his fingers began to move across the keyboard. He blinked and looked at the screen. There, in all caps, was the single word ANORA.

Bewildered, Bret gazed at the computer screen. Then, from somewhere in the house, he heard the low, muffled sound of crying. He jumped to his feet, the computer clattering to the floor.

Bret smiled at his own jumpiness. That's just the wind, he thought. He walked to the window and looked out at the tree growing next to the house.

"That's odd," he mused. In the moonlight he could see the leaves of the old, gnarled tree, hanging limp, there was no wind.

Again he heard the strange sound. He looked around the room. The sobbing noise seemed to be coming from upstairs. Must be a bunch of pigeons roosting up there, he thought. But it doesn't sound like any pigeons I've ever heard. He shook his head. These old houses, he reasoned, sometimes distort sounds. That must be it. Maybe it's some sort of animal, maybe a hungry one.

I better check it out. Don't want anything crawling in the sleeping bag with me in the middle of the night.

Bret took a candle from the mantle and walked through the archway to the foot of the staircase. A shiver ran up his spine as the sound grew louder. He took a deep breath. Take it easy, he admonished himself. Don't let this place get to you. But in spite of his logical self-reassurance, to him, the sound seemed unmistakable. It could only be the weeping of a woman in torment.

Slowly he mounted the steps and peered into the darkness at the top of the landing. The ancient treads creaked under his weight as he haltingly moved upward.

He was halfway up the stairway when he suddenly stopped, frozen in place. A chilling sensation washed over his body as his heart began to race and his knees weakened.

"Holy shit!" he cried aloud, grabbing the banister for support.

At the head of the stairs he saw a woman in a floor-length white dress with a full skirt. It was not a hoop skirt but one from a much earlier period. She was not transparent, just a white silhouette, and Bret could not make out the woman's features. He stared at her, transfixed, for several seconds. Then she was gone. There was no gradual fading away. One instant she was there. The next she wasn't.

Bret shook his head, took a deep breath, and turned back toward the downstairs landing. He had taken only a few steps when the crying resumed. This time it was more of a wailing than gentle sobbing. The chilling sensation returned. He didn't want to look back, but he couldn't restrain himself.

She was there again, at the top of the stairs. Now he could see her features, her face a mask of agonizing torment. Bret suddenly felt an overpowering feeling of sadness as compassion for the apparition swelled within him. With tears streaming down her cheeks, she beckoned for him to come to her.

As he approached the figure again disappeared, like the light from a bulb suddenly switched off. When he reached the landing he stood for a moment, surveying the hall leading to the bedrooms on the third floor.

He whirled as the sound of weeping began anew. The crying woman was standing by a door at the end of the hall, a pleading expression on her chalk-white face. As Bret slowly walked toward her the figure faded and the door swung slowly open. The rasping creak of the hinges sent a chill up his spine.

He thrust the candle through the doorway. There were more stairs. Slowly he made his way upward. At the top of the steps he held the candle high over his head. He was in the attic.

The weeping began again, softly, almost inaudible. Bret turned in the direction of the sobs. Across the cluttered garret he saw an old trunk against the far wall. Moonlight streaming through the round, louvered vent above it thrust the chest into an eerie prominence as it sat in a milky pool on the dusty floor.

Putting the candle on a nearby box Bret knelt and took hold of the lid and tried to lift it. It was locked. Now the trunk was shimmering with a ghostly glow that didn't seem to be generated by the pale moonlight or flickering candle.

Bret rose and looked around for something to pry open the lid. He jerked his head back toward the trunk when he heard the click. The lid was ajar.

When he raised the lid of the chest a gust of musty air rushed upward, the stench nearly gagging him. He stepped back and waved his hand in front of his face to dissipate the stench. Then, slowly, he approached the chest and knelt again.

Gingerly he took out what had once been a fine dress, but now a putrid, rotting rag. He draped it over the side of the trunk and picked up another. The white silk had yellowed with time and the brocade on the bodice was crumbling to dust.

At the bottom of the trunk he saw a rectangular wooden object he took to be a crude picture frame. He touched the wood. It was oak, its ancient grain raised and rough to the touch.

When he picked it up he discovered the object was a canvas stretcher, the canvas still attached. This must be an old painting, he thought. Somebody must have stored it here a long time ago. He rubbed the tip of his fingers over the canvas. Strange, he thought, as old as the wood is, and with these rusty tacks this canvas should be rotten. But it isn't. In fact, it looks new. He walked to the light of the candle and turned the canvas over.

He gasped as he saw staring at him from the painting the woman he had seen on the stairs. It was a somber painting, a composition of blacks, grays, and dirty whites. The expression on her face reflected the accumulated sadness of centuries.

Well, he thought, I see why someone put this monstrosity away in a trunk. That's where it belongs. And that's where it'll stay.

As he walked toward the trunk the lid slammed shut. He jumped aback and grinned at his own timidity. But when he tried to open the chest it was locked tight. No amount of tugging could lift the lid.

"O.K.," he said aloud. "I'll just leave it here with all this other junk." He leaned the painting against the trunk and turned toward the door.

A wailing rent the air as the specter of the woman appeared, blocking the door. She raised her arm slowly and pointed a trembling finger at the painting.

"You want me to take this with me?" Bret asked, the chilling feeling again washing over him. My God, he thought, I'm talking to a ghost. He closed his eyes and shook his head violently. Slowly he opened his eyes, expecting the apparition to be gone. It wasn't. Again she pointed to the painting and nodded. In a daze, he walked to the painting and picked it up. A slight smile came to the woman's lips and the door swung slowly open. As Bret neared the door, the painting under his arm, the phantom stepped aside and was gone. Shaken, barely able to move, he put his trembling hand on the knob. My God, he thought, what's happening?

* * * * *

Bret stood in the middle of the parlor, the painting dangling from his hand. With his other hand he wiped the perspiration from his forehead. He looked down at the painting and shook his head.

That couldn't have really happened, he silently assured himself. It's got to be some kind of hallucination brought on by the surroundings in this old place. He smiled. And that load of crap Mama Daka gave me about the place probably had a lot to do with it, too, he reasoned.

Bret walked to the fireplace, put the painting on the mantel, and stepped back. Well, he thought as he scrutinized it, you're one ugly piece of crap. A low moan, not of sorrow but of contentment, rumbled through the room. Bret looked around apprehensively. He was completely alone, alone with the flickering candles, somber shadows, and the grotesque painting.

CHAPTER 3

With the coming of dawn the eerie mantle that hung over Halfrith Hall by night faded. Sunlight streamed through the windows and crept across the floors. The dust of countless years hung in the air, shimmering in the rays of the morning sun.

Bret Kenway stirred and sat up. Rubbing the sleep from his eyes, he looked around. The sleeping bag lay unused in front of the fireplace. He had fallen asleep on the couch and slept in his clothes. He got to his feet and stood for a moment looking out the window at the gnarled tree. He shrugged, thinking it didn't look nearly so spooky by daylight. He stretched and groaned softly. His body was sore from the night spent on the lumpy couch. Gingerly, he rubbed the crick in his neck. Turning to the painting, he tossed a flippant salute in its direction.

"Good morning, you ugly piece of crap," he said. "You look as bad as I feel."

Rubbing his back with both hands, he turned and went downstairs to the kitchen.

Sleepily, he walked to the breakfront in the corner of the room. He couldn't help but think the plastic water bottles looked out of place on the marble top of the ornately carved piece of furniture. He grinned and filled the porcelain washbasin from one of the bottles. Taking a deep breath, he scooped up the water and splashed it on his face.

* * * * *

After his morning grooming he took a praline from the bag on the kitchen table. This will hold me for awhile, he thought. I'll get a little work done before I go into town for breakfast.

As he mounted the stairs leading to the second floor he heard women's voices coming from the parlor. Who's that, he thought. I don't know any women around here. Hell, I don't know *anybody* around here, men or women. He cocked this ear toward the upstairs. The voices were definitely feminine, but low and muffled. He couldn't make out what they were saying. Maybe, he thought, Landry has found a buyer for the place and sent his receptionist to evict me. And it sounds like she's brought a couple of friends.

* * * * *

When Bret reached the second floor landing the voices abruptly stopped. He walked into the parlor and found it empty. He listened intently but heard nothing. A quick search of the rest of the house proved fruitless. He could find no one.

Bret walked back into the parlor and glanced at his watch. Hell, he thought, that was a waste of time. It's nearly ten o'clock. Might as well drive into town and get some breakfast.

* * * * *

It was nearly noon when Bret returned to Halfrith Hall. He went to the parlor, sat on the couch, and opened his laptop.

"O.K.," he said, glancing at the painting on the mantle, "looks like it's just you and me. Time to get to work."

Bret's casual glance became a concentrated stare as he slowly closed his laptop and set it aside. There's something different about that painting, he thought. He peered intently at it for a moment, then shook his head. Naw, he told himself, it's still the same ugly piece of crap. It's just the light in here.

Bret rose and slowly walked to the painting. Again he shook his head. "No," he said aloud in a soft tone, "it's not just the light. Something is different."

The rose in a vase on a table next to the woman was no longer a muddy gray. It now had a slight, almost imperceptible tinge of pink. He studies the painting closely. The woman's hair, that just this morning had been a charcoal-black, was lighter. Her gray skin was also changing; now almost the color of living flesh and bits of color were creeping into the somber background of the painting.

Bret looked toward the window, at the rays of sunlight filtering through the grimy panes of glass and falling on the painting. He raised his hand and passed it through the beams. Huh, he thought, a strange angle for this time of day. The sun should be almost overhead now. But the light seems to be coming almost parallel to the floor. He shrugged. The windows in this old place are beveled glass, he told himself. They must be refracting the light, he concluded. Gently, he pressed his fingertips to the surface of the painting. Withdrawing his hand, he studied the tips of his fingers. They were dry, not oily as he had expected. He had thought, perhaps, the warmth of the sun had caused color under the somber painting to bleed through. But since the surface of the painting was completely dry he dismissed the theory.

Bret walked back to the couch, sat, and picked up his laptop. Glancing back at the painting, he smiled. Well, he thought, I don't know what's happening here. But you just gave me the title for this book. Quickly he typed the title in bold caps, THE WOMAN IN THE PAINTING.

* * * * *

Over the next few days when Bret was out of the parlor he heard female voices coming from there. Each time he entered, they stopped. With each passing day he noticed further subtle changes in the portrait over the mantle. The colors were becoming more vivid.

Within a week the painting had undergone a complete transformation. It now revealed a pretty, blue-eyed, redheaded young woman. She sat in a blue velvet upholstered chair. The vase on the table at her side had turned pale amber and the roses a vibrant pink.

The lady in the painting was now a far cry from the black, gray, and muddy white she had been only a week ago. But there was a haunting sadness in her eyes that seized and held Bret's gaze when he looked at her. To avoid the disturbing gaze, several times he turned the portrait to the wall. But each time he was suddenly overwhelmed with a deep sense of guilt and he returned the picture to its original position. He could no longer keep his mind on his work. His thoughts were dominated by the woman in the painting.

* * * * *

After three days of writer's block he decided something had to be done about the situation. But what? Although he felt a little foolish about it, he decided to go to the only person he knew that might have some sort of explanation for what was happening.

* * * * *

Mama Daka stood with Bret in the parlor squinting at the painting.

"Good you come to me, mon," she said. "This very bad magic. This work of devil mon, Perrin Fortier."

"The one who painted the picture of . . . " Bret paused, pursed his lips, and snapped his finger several times. "What was her name?" he asked.

"Anora Baker, mon."

At the mention of the name Bret felt a strange, sinking feeling in the pit of his stomach. He recalled the almost forgotten incident of a few days ago when, for no apparent reason, he had typed the name on his computer. At the time he didn't know why. But now it made sense in an uncanny way and it made him uneasy.

Could it be, he wondered, Anora's spirit had directed his fingers? Had she been waiting over two hundred years for his arrival? Quickly he dismissed the thought as nonsense.

"You're saying," Bret asked Mama Daka, "this is a portrait of her?" The voodoo priestess nodded. "That would mean this painting is over two hundred years old," Bret said, disbelief in his voice. "But it sure doesn't look like it. The canvas is new, and there are no age cracks in the paint. And considering how it was stored, a two hundred year old painting wouldn't be in this good a condition."

Mama Daka glared at Bret. "Then how you explain what happen, mon?" she asked.

Bret shook his head. "I can't," he admitted.

"You want Mama Daka tell you what happen?"

"Sure."

"You remember I tell you devil mon, Fortier, send young woman, Anora Baker, to place she no come back from?"

"Yes."

"He kill her and send her through picture he be painting. Lock her spirit away in bad place. Picture like door to other world. Or maybe window. She can look through but no can come back, have stay on other side. He put picture in trunk where you find it."

Bret looked at the painting, then back to the voodoo priestess. Slowly he shook his head and smiled.

"That's a little hard to believe," he said.

"What you think, mon?" the woman spat through clenched teeth. "You think you know more about this than Mama Daka?"

"No, but . . . "

"You be quiet and listen, mon. Anora Baker have power turn picture all black and ugly because she no like where it be. When you put on mantle, in sunlight, she bring color back."

"But," Bret insisted, "why me? There must have been lots of people living in this house over the last two hundred years. Why didn't they find it? It wasn't hidden very well. It was just at the bottom of an old trunk in the attic."

Mama Daka put her hand on Bret's shoulder. "But," she said, "they not stay long. They leave when Anora try bring them to attic like you." The voodoo priestess grinned. "They not brave like you," she concluded.

"In those days, I suppose, people believed in ghosts more than today, and were easily frightened. Are you saying they were scared out of the house before they ever went into the attic?"

"That it, mon." Mama Daka looked at the painting. "Now," she asked, "what you do with picture?"

"Do?" Bret repeated. "What do you think I should do with it?"

"Better you put it back where you find it. You no can help Anora Baker now, she long time dead."

"Well, I don't know. It seems a shame to put her back in the trunk." Bret flinched. My God, he thought, listen to me. I'm talking about a painting as if it were a living person.

His fit of reason was short-lived. A small voice deep within his being reminded him of the picture's miraculous transformation.

"Why not leave her there over the mantle?" he suggested. "She seems to like it there."

"No, mon, that not good. Better you not look at picture too much."

"Why not?"

"Devil mon Fortier's magic in picture. If you no get rid of it maybe you, too, go place where no can come back." Mama Daka cast another glance at the painting. "I go now," she announced, sweeping her arm in the direction of the mantle. "I no stay here with that."

* * * * *

Bret stood on the porch watching Mama Daka drive away in her battered old car. Soon she disappeared in a trail of dust from the rutted driveway leading to the main road. The sun was setting and long shadows cast by the gnarled trees began to creep across the ground. Bret looked at the blazing red sun slowly sinking below the western horizon.

He sat on the steps and pondered what Mama Daka had told him. He didn't want to believe a word of it. Had he been told such a story only a few weeks ago he would have laughingly dismissed it as superstitious nonsense. But since it had happened to him, he had no choice but to believe it.

* * * * *

Bret watched the gray twilight turn to darkness. A sudden chill sent a shiver up his spine. Damn, he thought, how could I be cold in Louisiana in the middle of summer? He rubbed his arms briskly and rose. When he turned and moved a few steps toward the front door the chill left him. He was now in the warm, humid surroundings typical of the season.

Bret shuddered. He had heard stories of haunted houses where cold spots existed in an otherwise warm room. According to the stories they were supposed to indicate the presence of a ghost.

"Bullshit," Bret murmured aloud. Then he went into the house and climbed the stairs to the parlor.

* * * * *

Bret sat looking at the painting of Anora Baker. His laptop sat nearby but he made no effort to use it. Slowly he rose and walked to the mantle. In response to an urge he didn't understand, he gently moved the two candles closer to the portrait. He smiled as the flickering light cast soft shadows on Anora's face. He heaved a heavy sigh, turned and walked back to the couch and sat. Slumping, he stared at the floor in front of him. Then, as if by command from some unseen force, he turned to face the painting.

The woman's eyes shone with a phosphorescent light. He wanted to turn away, but couldn't. Suddenly a chilling fear stabbed at his heart. Bret wanted to flee, to get out of the house and as far away as possible. But his body would not respond. He felt like a rag doll, the sawdust within it slowly running out through an unseen gash, his body growing flat and useless. His heart pounded. His pulse raced. His knees began to tremble.

My god, he thought, I think I'm going to pass out. But, somehow, he didn't care. Transfixed, he continued to stare into the eyes of the woman in the painting.

Then from their azure blue emerged two rays that flowed into each other and swelled into a glowing circle.

Bret leaned back on the couch and exhaled slowly. The feeling of fear was gradually being replaced by a mind numbing euphoria. He was falling under the spell of the mysterious woman in the painting, and, strangely, he welcomed it.

Slowly a fine mist formed within the painting and issued outward. It billowed into a fleecy cloud, cascaded to the floor, and began spreading across the room.

The white glowing mist crept toward the couch, rising to the tall ceiling, filling the room. Now Bret could not see the painting. He grinned foolishly as the cloud enveloped him in a cool, soothing blanket. Before him he saw only the billowy cloud tinges with sparkling flecks of luminescent blue. Then all went black. He felt nothing, saw nothing, heard nothing.

CHAPTER 4

Adrift in the tranquil sea of blackness, Bret gradually became aware of a rushing sound. I wish that noise would stop, he thought. It's going to spoil everything. Go away, he commanded, leave me alone.

In spite of Bret's admonishment the sound did not go away, but steadily grew in intensity. Then bits of reality began asserting themselves, crowding into his muddled mind. Slowly the realization came to him. What he was hearing was the sound of howling wind. Then the sound of torrents of rain gave Bret another cruel prod back toward reality. Slowly he became aware of a subtle damp cold creeping into his body.

The sound of the wind and rain were encroaching on his dream world, and he tried to ignore them. He wanted to remain in the friendly mist that embraced him. But he wished it were a little warmer. The cold was beginning to dispel his feeling of complete contentment and he could no longer ignore the howling wind and falling rain. Then, as if from far away, he heard the women's voices.

"Does he still live?" one said. "Or was the transference more than he could bear?"

"I hope we didn't kill him with our summons," another said. "We've waited so long for this chance."

"How strangely he's dressed," said a third. "Those clothes will never do. He'll need ones that protect against the raw, damp cold."

"He shivers," the first voice said. "Wrap him in this."

Bret felt the hands on his shoulders, lifting him to a sitting position. Then he felt the warmth of something being wrapped around him. He opened his eyes and his vision slowly returned.

For a moment Bret sat in silent awe of his strange surroundings. He was on a dirt floor in the center of a tiny, windowless hovel. The walls were of mud and overhead exposed beams supported a thatched shed roof badly in need of repair. Rain ran through bare spots in the roof, forming puddles on the dirt floor. In one corner of the small room was a crude fireplace. And although a roaring fire blazed there it did little to dispel the cold in the room.

The women were crouched on the floor looking into Bret's face. One was dark with long, straight black hair that framed her sunken brown eyes and high cheekbones as it fell to her shoulders. Her small breasts suggested early puberty, but her face proclaimed she was a woman who had endured much. Merciful death had ended her unbearable suffering on the earthly plane but could not erase the memory of it from her mind. The unspeakable torture she had endured was now reflected in her gaunt face.

The other woman was slightly older, and a complete contrast to the first. She was in her early twenties, rather stout, with round, firm breasts. She had deep blue eyes and sensuous pouting lips. Her blonde hair was cut short, giving her the look of a pixy.

Suddenly Bret realized he was wrapped in a wool blanket, being cradled in someone's arms. He looked up to see Anora Baker, the woman in the painting, smiling down at him. He issued a soft groan of contentment and snuggled closer to her breast.

"That one's not hurt at all," said the woman with the pixy haircut. "He still has every man's God-given appreciation for a soft bosom to lay his head on. And it's been my experience that them that don't are dead."

"This is some kind of crazy dream," Bret said. "I'll wake up any minute now. Might as well enjoy it while I can." He looked at the two women kneeling before him. "I just hope I can remember enough details to use this in my book," he told them. "By the way," he asked, "where the hell am I?"

"Call this place what you will," the thin, dark-haired woman said. "Gehenna would be appropriate for it is a land of sorrow and torment. We live in a dismal twilight for day and bone chilling darkness at night, lit only by a waxing moon that never changes. And the driving rains and cutting winds are all too frequent."

"It's as though Satan has the land enfolded in his wings, blocking out the light," the blonde woman added.

"It's always dark?" Bret asked.

"We've heard rumors that somewhere faraway from here there is light," Anora said. "But no one dares roam in search of such a place. His spawn are everywhere."

"His spawn?" Bret repeated questioningly. "Who's spawn?"

"The ruler of this land," Anora said. "He has set every manner of vile creature to roam the countryside and prey on unwary travelers. But never mind that now, we must lay plans. The tormentors may descend upon us at any time."

"The who?" Bret asked.

"The minions of the evil one who rules this land," Anora said. "They have the bodies of men but the hairy faces of warthogs. They're always gnashing their tusks, and when they talk they slobber. The wanton stare of their beady red eyes chills you to the bone. These foul creatures were created by the evil one with only one purpose, to abuse and torment us constantly."

"Can't you do something about it?" Bret asked. "There must be more of you than them around here. Can't you fight back?"

"We are powerless alone," the thin, dark woman said. "That's why we summoned you."

"Speaking of that," Bret said, "how did I get here? The last thing I remember was a sort of cloud . . . "

"We were responsible for that," Anora said.

"We?" Bret repeated. He sat up and looked at the three women. "Who is we?"

"This is Yolette Bettencourt," Anora said, pointing to the dark woman. "And this is Nelda Farnham," she added, indicating the blonde woman in the same manner. "It was our voices you heard in your world, just before we transported you." Anora smiled. "You have no idea how long we've been waiting for someone to find the painting."

"But why three of you?" Bret asked Anora. "The picture was only of you."

"Yes," she said. "Nelda's and Yolette's portraits were destroyed. So when you found mine in the attic of the house we combined our thoughts, hoping, with your help, to end our existence on this plain."

Bret looked at Anora, then the other two women. "This plain?" he questioned.

"The physical world you know is only one part of reality," Yolette said. "The border between the worlds of light and shadows is, paradoxically, hard to find but easily crossed."

"But, Bret asked, "what do you want from me?"

"You can help us leave this plain of torturous limbo," Anora said, "and find our final resting place, whether it be heaven or hell."

"How can I help you do that?" Bret asked.

Anora looked deep into his eyes as the other women pressed forward.

"You must destroy the evil one who reigns over this accursed kingdom," she said.

"Me? Why me? Why not you or someone else from around here?"

"Even if we could find his castle atop the mountain in the center of the lake of fire he would detect our approach from miles away."

"How?" Bret asked.

Yolette took Bret's hand. "All who inhabit this woeful plain were his victims," she said. "Our earthly lives were snatched from us by him. In this world of his own making he has complete dominion over us. But since you were not one of his victims he can not detect your presence from afar. Your life force puts you nearly on an even footing with him."

"Nearly?" Bret questioned with an apprehensive look. "What do you mean, nearly?"

"You are not a magician like he is," Nelda said. "But you have a special ability to approach undetected."

"Maybe he wouldn't see me coming," Bret said. "But I have a feeling he's going to have a lot of bodyguards hanging around. And to kill him I'd need to get through them."

"Not kill," Yolette corrected him, "destroy the evil one. You can't kill one who is already dead."

"Well," Bret said, "that'll make it even harder. If this, whatever he is, is already dead, what can I do to harm him?"

"There are things that will hurt him," Nelda said. "Things that will cause the devil to desert him."

"What kind of things?" Bret asked.

"The fatal blow to him would be the burning of his book of shadows."

"What?"

"His grimoire," Yolette said. "His book of spells. Every sorcerer, witch, and warlock has one. It is the source of their power. But it is said that one who rules this accursed place is not a fallen mortal in league with Satan but a devil from hell and his grimoire is sanctioned and signed by Satan himself."

"If the book should ever leave his possession," Nelda said, "it would cripple him. And if it were burned he would be completely stripped of his power."

"And then," Anora said, "because he is sustained only by the evil power of Satan whom he serves, his power over us would disappear."

"And then what?" Bret asked. "Does everyone here just evaporate? Or do you go back to where you were before you were sent here?"

Anora shrugged. "We honestly don't know," she said. "But we do know we will no longer languish here."

"How do you know?" Bret asked.

"Yolette and others have said so."

"Oh well then," Bret said sarcastically, "then that must be what will happen."

The look of hurt that came to Anora's face made Bret regret the remark.

"I'm sorry," he said. "How am I supposed to, as you say, destroy this character?"

"We won't lie to you," Yolette said. "This devil is very powerful. He roams the earth on one plain sending victims to this hellish place that he rules to be his subjects. And he abuses us most cruelly here. Who knows what other plains of existence he inhabits?

"He is ageless, presenting himself on the earthly plain as different people in different times. I met him when the inquisition begun in Spain made its way to France. He was masquerading as an inquisitor known as Gano Cuvier. To Nelda he was a tavern keeper in Port-au-Prince. There, in that time, he was called Auburt Guignard. And to Anora he represented himself as a painter by the name of Perrin Fortier.

"His magic is powerful. But he is not the only one who practices the black arts here. And there are a few like myself who practice white magic, the art of Wicca."

"If this ruler is so omnipotent, and can apparently know what's happening everywhere, why does he let anyone practice magic? Seems to me he wouldn't want any competition in that area."

"None are powerful enough to go against him alone and he knows it. But he enjoys pitting practitioners of the black arts against one another in the annual reckoning held in his castle."

"What's that?"

"It's a battle of wizards by demon proxies. Any who wish to enter the competition must make the perilous journey to the castle, arriving on the Eve of Sambain. Many don't survive the trip; as they are set upon by his evil spawn that roam the countryside. They are especially powerful and ravenous on the Eve of Sambain."

"What's this Eve of Sambain?" Bret asked.

"The ancient Druids celebrated Sambain, or 'summer's end' with human sacrifices, augury, and prayer. Spirits were thought to gather when the sun began to set and hovered about all through the night as natural laws were suspended."

"Sounds like Halloween," Bret said.

"Later the celebration became Hallow E'en," Nelda said. "And eventually Halloween. But here, believe me, it's taken a lot more seriously than in your world."

"Sounds like it," Bret mused.

"Once the wizards are assembled," Yolette continued, "each conjures up a demon to do battle with those of the other wizards. Sometimes the fighting goes on for hours as they tear each other to pieces. The master of the last demon standing is the winner of the reckoning. For the next year they enjoy the privilege of sitting at the right hand of the evil one who rules this land."

Suddenly Yolette fell silent, her head cocked, listening intently. "They come," she said. "Quickly, into the secret place. It is my turn to deal with the tormentors."

Anora took Bret by the hand and led him to the wall of the hovel. With Nelda's help she moved aside two sacks of grain, revealing a hole in the floor, the top of a ladder protruding just above the dirt rim.

"Down into the dugout, quickly," Nelda said.

"But what about her?" Bret asked, pointing to Yolette. "We can't just leave her alone to deal with whatever's coming."

"We have to," Anora said.

"If the tormentors find an empty place they burn it down," Nelda said. "Better one of us take the abuse and keep a roof over our heads."

"But," Bret persisted.

"Quickly!" Yolette screamed, "get hidden. They are nearly at the door."

Reluctantly Bret descended into the darkness of the hiding place. Anora and Nelda followed and the three stood huddled together in the small pit. Once they were inside Yolette replaced the grain bags, concealing the opening.

* * * * *

Yolette had moved to the center of the hovel when the door burst open and four husky figures walked in. They wore black leather armor with rusty iron studs, the familiar dress of the tormentors. Scraggly beards hid most of their warthog faces except for their curved tusks and red bulging beady eyes. Contemptuously the tormentors looked around.

"You are alone?" one asked. Before Yolette could reply he sneered and added, "Or are there other vermin such as you lurking nearby?"

"As you can see," Yolette answered meekly, "I'm quite alone here."

"You wouldn't lie to me would you?"

"Never," Yolette replied with a catch in her voice. "I would never lie to representatives of the ruler."

Another tormentor standing at Yolette's side grabbed her by the chin. Roughly he jerked her head to the side and shoved his face within inches of hers. For an instant he glared at her, his pig eyes bulging. Then with a snort of disgust he shoved the palm of his hand into her face and pushed her away.

"This house is no good for our quest," he said. "Our mission is to bring the ruler young women for his pleasure."

"You're right," the first tormentor said. "This skinny scarecrow will not do. We'll have to look elsewhere."

The first tormentor grabbed Yolette roughly by the shoulder and spun her around to face him. Grinning sadistically, he lashed out with a hard right jab to her mouth. His companions laughed as she crumpled to the floor.

"That's for wasting our time, you hag," he said. Again the others laughed. Then the tormentors left, slamming the door behind them.

*****

Bret and the women emerged from their hiding place to see Yolette sitting on the floor a trickle of blood running from the corner of her mouth and down her chin. When she saw them she bowed her head and began to weep, her fingers clawing helplessly at the dirt floor. They ran to her side and helped her to her feet.

"Why the hell did you take me into that hole in the ground to hide while this poor girl took a beating?" Bret asked, his voice tinged with rage. "If I'd known what was going to happen I'd have stayed with her. I might not have been able to prevent it. But those bastards would have had a harder time pushing me around than a defenseless girl."

"That would have accomplished nothing but your death," Anora told him. "And who would help us in our plan then?"

Bret shrugged and nodded. "I guess that makes sense," he said. "But it still doesn't set right with me to hide while a woman is being mistreated."

"That's the situation here," Nelda said to Bret. "Each time those brutes come here one of us takes the brunt of their evil pleasures while the others hide. The physical torture is fleeting and we have grown accustomed to it. But it's heartbreaking to see the mental torture heaped on poor Yolette."

Bret looked at Yolette still sobbing softly while Anora tried to comfort her.

"Those bastards are going to pay for this," he said. Then, turning to Nelda, he asked, "How do I get to this damned castle in the middle of the burning lake? And who can I count on to go with me?"

CHAPTER 5

"We'd all like to go with you," Anora said. "But our presence would be sensed by the evil one."

"Then the element of surprise would be lost," Nelda added. "And without that you wouldn't stand a chance of success."

"Well now," Bret said, "let's give this thing a little thought. You tell me people go into the castle every year. And they don't have to sneak in."

"You don't mean . . . " Yolette began.

"Right," Bret cut her off. "I'll walk into the castle as part of the annual reckoning." He grinned at the women. "With my three able assistants, or course," he added.

"It would be a dangerous masquerade," Yolette warned. "Without at least some power you'll be naked before the other sorcerers there. If you are unable to create a demon to take part in the mayhem, theirs may turn on you."

"I don't intend to match spells with them. But you'll have to teach me some of the lingo so I can bluff my way into the castle. Once inside we'll search for his grimoire. He's bound to be occupied with the battle of wizards and shouldn't miss a few people."

"The reckoning is within a month," Yolette said. "We have much to do before then."

"One of the first things," Nelda said, "is to get you into some warm clothes. You can't go around wrapped in a blanket."

"I'll make it into a robe for him," Anora said. "When I'm finished no one will recognize it as a blanket."

"And I'll begin your instruction in Wicca," Yolette said. "Of course we have not near enough time to teach you any real knowledge. But enough for you to learn a few phrases that will convince the tormentors you are a real sorcerer."

"You'll need a sword and dagger," Nelda said. "And a wand too, I should think. No self-respecting sorcerer would be caught without one. I can supply the sword and dagger." A faraway look came to Nelda's eyes. "Heaven knows," she said softly, "I'll have no need of them here."

"And I can fix something that will pass for a wand," Yolette said. "Of course, none of these things will have any power as you aren't a real sorcerer. But they will complete your disguise."

"Now let me have the blanket," Anora said. "I'll start sewing it right away."

Bret handed the blanket to Anora. "Damn, it's cold here," he said. "If I'd known I was coming here I'd have put on something warmer than this short sleeved cotton shirt."

Nelda smiled and took Bret by the arm. "Don't worry," she told him, "I'll keep you warm till your new robe is finished." The other two women smiled knowingly as she led him toward the bed in the corner.

* * * * *

Over the next few days Bret spent a lot of time with Yolette, often studying late into the night. At times he was pleased to see a slight smile on her lips. He had hoped that in the course of their conversations she would volunteer further information about herself and the other two women, but she never did. Finally, unable to withstand the gnawing curiosity any longer, he decided to broach the subject.

Anora and Nelda were asleep. Yolette and Bret sat before the fireplace engaged in their nightly lesson.

"Tell me about yourself and your two friends," he said.

"What do you want to know?" Yolette asked.

"Everything. Where you were born, what you did while you were growing up, and, if it's not too painful, how you came to be here."

"Why do you want to know that?" she asked.

"Call it writer's curiosity. I'm interested."

"You are interested in me?" Yolette asked, flushing with embarrassment.

"Yes," Bret assured her with a broad smile.

"But I'm so plain and unattractive. Even as a child people said . . ."

Bret put his finger to Yolette's lips silencing her. "You are not plain or unattractive," he told her. "Oh sure, you don't have flashy good looks like some women. But that's usually superficial and pretty boring after awhile. Pretty is a dime a dozen. But character is something else."

Yolette looked puzzled. "I don't understand that phrase," she said. "What is a dime?"

"It means that outward beauty is not hard to find and usually not worth much. But character is rare and precious when found."

Yolette blushed. "You think I have character?" she asked.

"You're loaded with it," Bret replied. "And, in your own way, you're very pretty. I know lots of women that would kill for your eyes and high cheekbones. In my world you would be considered a perfect high fashion model."

"You're teasing me," Yolette said, casting her eyes downward.

"No," Bret insisted, "it's true. That's why I want to know more about you."

Yolette smiled. "All right," she began, "I'll tell you about myself. But as for Anora and Nelda, they'll have to tell you their story themselves."

"I already know a little about Anora. And I want to know about Nelda. But right now I really want to hear about you."

Yolette smiled and moved closer to Bret. In a low voice she began her tale.

* * * * *

Yolette Bettencourt was born November 11, 1217 in the small village of Trevol near Lyon France. She grew up in the peaceful surroundings of the green hills near the confluence of the Rhone and Saone Rivers. Being the youngest of seven children she entertained herself with long walks in the hills. There she sat and watched the rivers flow south toward Marseille to empty into the Mediterranean Sea or lay on the grass and look up at the constantly changing shaped of the clouds.

When Yolette was ten years old, as she sat on a hillside overlooking the river, she noticed an old woman walking along its bank. She kept her eyes fixed on the ground in front of her as she walked, halting frequently to bend down and pick a plant and put it in the small wicker basket she carried on her arm. As the woman drew near Yolette spoke.

"Good morning," she said cheerfully. The woman looked up startled, then smiled and nodded. "I'm Yolette Bettencourt," the young girl continued. "I live in the village just over there." Yolette rose and started toward the woman. "I don't believe I've seen you in these hills before," she went on. "May I ask your name?"

The woman scowled. "Madame Sibyla," she said curtly as though Yolette should know her.

Of course Yolette had heard the name before. She had been told of the old female recluse that lived in a cave somewhere in the hills outside the village. There were those who believed she was a witch. But Yolette's father had told her and the other children she was not. He explained that she was just an unfortunate old soul who had lost her husband, children, and home in a fire years ago.

For a while she lived off the charity of the other villagers. But soon her pride drove her from the town to live in a cave, sustaining herself with berries, nuts, and other eatable plants from the woods.

"Do you come here often?" Yolette asked.

"I roam these hills at my pleasure," Madame Sibyla said. "It is my apothecary." Proudly she showed Yolette the basket of plants and herbs.

"What do you do with them?" Yolette asked.

"I make healing potions and such." The woman smiled at Yolette. "What did you think?" she asked. "Did you think I used them to cast evil spells?"

Yolette shook her head. "No," she said.

"People say I'm an evil witch you know."

"Some do, but not all. My father says you aren't."

Madame Sibyla grinned. "He's a very intelligent man," she said. "You should listen to him." Yolette nodded. "As a matter of fact," Sibyla went on, "I am a witch." Yolette's eyes widened, more in wonder than fear. Madame Sibyla chuckled. "But not an evil one," she said. "I practice the white magic of Wicca."

"What's that?" Yolette wanted to know.

"We believe in the healing spirit of nature, among other things most find strange." Madame Sibyla looked deeply into Yolette's eyes. "Would you like to learn about Wicca?" she asked.

"I don't know . . . I've never . . . "

"My arcane senses tell me you carry the seed of the power within you," Madame Sibyla said. "It only needs to be nurtured." She put her hand on Yolette's head. "Wicca asks nothing of you but you approach with an open mind," she said. "Reject nothing on the basis of previously learned ideas, but weigh each new pronouncement on its own merits."

Suddenly Yolette felt a strange presence, instinctively knowing whatever it was to be very ancient and wise and definitely female. She felt as though this presence was looking down on her with infinite love and patience.

* * * * *

For the next three years Madame Sibyla instructed Yolette in the white magic art of Wicca. The young girl found that embracing Wicca was not a process of instant conversion but one of slow, steady self-persuasion. The craft did not command immediate commitment nor were there any set of preordained beliefs for the novice to put into practice. Since the Wicca creed flew in the face of convention, Yolette, like many initiates, needed to take time for a gradual growth of belief.

* * * * *

At the end of three years Yolette's apprenticeship to Madame Sibyla came to an end. And one night as they met on a moonlit hillside next to the river Yolette became a witch.

"I have taught you all I know about healing and other forms of magic," Madame Sibyla said. "You have mastered the Witches Garden. You know the healing plants and plants of protection as well as spellbinding plants. You have learned that Wicca identifies with the moon, symbolic of the Great Goddess in all her forms, Maiden, Mother, and Crone. We have performed together the ceremonies of Drawing Down the Moon and Raising the Cone of Power. Now kneel before me, it is time for your initiation."

Yolette knelt before Madame Sibyla. Walking slowly around the young girl, she drew a magic circle in the air with the sweep of her forefinger. Then she grasped Yolette's wrists, pulling her to her feet and turned her in four directions, presenting her to the four compass points. Yolette was now a full-fledged witch.

"Now go," Madame Sibyla said. "Go and use your power as I have taught you." Then she turned and walked away, leaving Yolette alone in the moonlight.

* * * * *

Yolette never again saw Madame Sibyla. It was rumored by some of the ignorant in the village that she flew off to a witches' Sabbath on the other side of the earth and never returned. Others reasoned that she had died of old age and exposure in her cave dwelling during the winter and her body eaten by wild animals. Others thought she had fallen into the river and drowned while gathering herbs on its bank. But to Yolette Madame Sibyla was not dead. She was ever with her in spirit as she went about the practice of Wicca.

* * * * *

Three years later, in 1233, when Yolette was still a young girl of sixteen, a reign of terror brought by the inquisition reached France. When the witch hunt struck a community its horrors dominated the lives of all its citizens. Torture and fear twisted truth into grotesque travesties and shattered loyalties. Brothers were forced to denounce brothers, wives their husbands, and peasants their lords.

Accusation was tantamount to conviction and all witches were convicted by confessions wrung from them by torture. Hopelessly trapped in the pitiless iron grip of a tribunal of inquisitors victims sought to end their suffering by confessing to whatever pleased their tormentors.

It made no difference to the inquisitors whether the accused was young, old, man, woman, or child. They would be subjected to unbearable agony until they confessed or died from the treatment. The inquisitors boasted they would gladly burn a hundred if just one among them were guilty.

* * * * *

Yolette, being a known practitioner of Wicca, was brought before the merciless council of inquisitors. She was charged with sorcery, murder, necromancy, and that she had denied God, defiled the sacraments, and performed demonic rituals. She was said to have been seen cavorting naked with a coven of demons on the hillsides under the full moon. She was also accused of taking demons of hideous form into her bed.

Dressed in the loosefitting white robe, forced on all accused, Yolette stood before the tribunal assembled in one of the many basement rooms of the village church. The area was mostly in shadows, the flickering torches casting eerie dancing shadows on the walls and floor. The air hung dank and heavy, permeated with the stench of fear and sweat.

Frightened, she looked pleadingly at the group seated before her and the two guards at her sides.

"Yolette Bettencourt," one of the men began in a somber tone, "you have been accused of witchcraft most vile. Do you now confess it of your own free will?"

"I am not guilty of any wrong," Yolette said.

"Are you not a practitioner of the art called Wicca?" the man shot back.

"Yes. But it is a healing art, not associated with black magic in any way."

"We'll be the judge of that." The man turned to his fellow inquisitors and conversed in low tones. Then he turned again to Yolette. "You will be given the opportunity to repent your evil liaison with the devil," he said. Then addressing the guards he ordered, "Take this woman to the solitary chamber."

* * * * *

The chamber Yolette was taken to was a smaller room in the far corner of the church basement below the kitchen. A few short months ago, before the madness of the inquisition, it had served as storage for potatoes and other vegetables as well as flour and millet. Now the floor was cluttered with torture devices and chains and manacles hung from every wall. The odor of the room's former use was gone and it now reeked of blood and death.

* * * * *

For two days Yolette was chained to the wall in the solitary chamber. It was windowless and the only light came from the brazier that was kept alive with glowing coals. At regular intervals guards came in to tend the fire. Sometimes they took hot irons from the brazier when they left and Yolette heard screams coming from other parts of the basement.

* * * * *

On the night of the second day the door swung open and a dark figure walked in. Yolette, weak from hunger and thirst, hung limp in the chains but managed to lift her head to look at him. He was a large man, dressed in a black robe and a hood that hid his features. For a long moment he stood looking at Yolette, then pushed back the hood, revealing his face. In the light of the torch he carried she recognized him as the chief inquisitor, the one who had ordered her here.

He put the torch in a metal ring on the wall above a small table. Then he opened his robe and took out an icon that Yolette recognized as one from the church altar. He studies it critically for an instant then sat it on the table. He turned to Yolette and smiled.

"I am Gano Cuvier," he said. "I am here to attend to your needs." He leered at Yolette and added, "And mine as well."

"Mercy," Yolette pleaded in a feeble voice. "Mercy. I have done nothing."

Gano Cuvier walked to Yolette and unlocked her manacles. She fell limp in his arms. He carried her to the rack and roughly threw her down. Then he mounted her, forced her legs apart, and savagely entered her.

* * * * *

When Gavo Cuvier had satisfied his lust he stood looking down at Yolette. A smirk came to his face as he took a garrote from under his robe.

"Yolette Bettencourt," he murmured in a sarcastic monotone, "I find you guilty of witchcraft. And I sentence you to death." He jerked her to a sitting position and stood behind her. Yolette was too weak to resist as Gano Cuvier applied the garrote, draining away any faint glimmer of life that remained in her tortured body. As she fell limp he looked down at her, then at the icon on the table. He passed his hands over the body and it began to fade, assuming the shape of a cloud. Gano Cuvier gestured in the direction of the icon. Instantly the cloud drifted toward it and disappeared within its frame.

Gano Cuvier took the icon from the table and tossed it into the burning brazier. For an instant it smoldered, black smoke rising. Then the dry, ancient wood and lacquer burst into flames.

* * * * *

Yolette sighed and looked into the dying embers of the fireplace. "And that's how I came to be here," she said. "I was a victim of the times I lived in. And the one who sent me here was the same one who sent us all here. He was my personal devil and known to me as Gano Cuvier. To the others he goes by another name, but is the same vile creature. And he now holds us all in his cruel grip."

Bret took Yolette's hand in his. "We're going to do something about that," he said. Yolette smiled but made no reply.

CHAPTER 6

The Eve of Sambain was fast approaching. Yolette had taught Bret all she could in the little time they had. Although he had no real occult powers, under her tutelage, he had learned to look and sound the part of a warlock. Yolette was confident he would be able to join in the reckoning without challenge. Now it was time to make the perilous trip to the castle atop the mountain in the lake of fire.

"Are you sure you know the way to this castle?" Bret asked the women. "I don't want to keep roaming around in this stinking weather forever."

"It sits under the waxing moon," Yolette replied. "We have only to steer by that and all roads lead to the lake of fire and the castle."

"Any idea how far it is?" Bret asked.

"No," Nelda replied. "But if we leave soon we should reach the castle in good time for the reckoning. And should we arrive early, we can join the others."

"The others?" Bret questioned.

"I am told there is always an encampment of wizards by the lake of fire," Yolette said. "Many arrive early, but are not allowed across till the Eve of Sambain."

"All right," Bret said. "We'll plan on leaving as soon as we get up from our next sleeping period."

* * * * *

Bret and the women stood at the door of the hovel slowly scanning the room for one last look. Outside, a cold mist swirled around the cabin driven by a low moaning wind. The thunderstorm had passed and small puddles of water glistened in the pale moonlight. The women had packed what meager possessions they had in small bundles that could be conveniently carried on their arm.

In his belt Bret carried Nelda's dagger. Yolette had darkened its handle with charcoal from the fireplace and told him to never refer to it as anything other than the athame. This was the proper term for the double-edged knife used by a sorcerer to direct personal power, or psychic energy, from their body out into the world.

The sword was another essential trapping of a wizard. It, like the athame, performed symbolic or psychic cutting. It was used to draw the magic circle, cutting off the encircled space from the ordinary world.

The symbolic sword of a sorcerer was usually a long, double-edged smaller version of the broadsword. But the only sword Nelda could provide was a single-edged cutlass. For appearances Bret would be wearing it when he entered the castle, but for now Nelda kept it. She had assured Bret she knew how to use the sword and would be the logical one to wield it if they ran into trouble.

Bret looked around the room. "Well," he said, "I don't suppose we'll be seeing this place again. If the tormentors come and find it empty they'll destroy it."

"Yes, they will," Yolette agreed. "But it doesn't matter. We won't be coming back here anyway."

"Let's hope not," Nelda said. "The only reason we would is if we fail in our mission."

"And if we do," Anora added, "I'd rather perish in the castle than come back here."

"Don't even think about failing," Bret admonished the woman. "Just keep thinking of how good it's going to feel to be free of that evil bastard that sent you here." The women smiled and nodded. "Now," Bret said, "let's get going."

"Before we go," Yolette said, "I have something to give each of you."

"What is it?" Anora questioned.

"The countryside is rampant with evil entities," Yolette told her. "So I have prepared talismans for all." She reached into her bundle and withdrew three brightly polished brass crescents attached to strings. "Wear these around your necks," she said as she handed them to her companions. "These will reflect ill-will back to its source. But you must keep them well burnished. Their power will weaken should you allow them to become corroded."

"What about you?" Anora asked. "You didn't make one for yourself."

"I'll be protected by this," Yolette replied, holding up the object suspended around her neck. "Notice this stone I chanced to find has a hole worn through it," she went on. "Such an object always brings the finder certain luck. To enhance its power I have attached an iron key to the stone. Iron, in all its forms, is a metal feared by most evil entities."

"I sure hope you're right," Bret said. "We're going to need all the help we can get."

* * * * *

The weather was cold and dreary as Bret and the women stepped outside the hovel and closed the door for the last time. Gray clouds hung low on the mountains obscuring their crests. The road was narrow and rocky, snaking its way into the hills ahead and disappearing into the mist.

* * * * *

As the trail rose above the valley into the hills the vegetation at its sides grew sparse. Soon the land became barren. The rocky trail ran by small glens strewn with boulders and through mountains of sheer stone rising into the clouds. Baleful creatures scurried and slithered at the side of the road, suspicion in their small, beady eyes as they watched the travelers. Ancient stone bridges, their approaches protected by brooding gargoyles, spanned deep gorges filled with dark swirling clouds. The mouths of tunnels, worn by long dead underground rivers, looked out on the trail where it ran close to the face of the cliff. Some were ragged gaping black holes, while others, shielded by overhanging rocks, were barely visible in the gloomy constant half-light.

As Bret and the women trudged upward along the narrow, rocky trail the clouds darkened and a fine mist began to fall.

"We better find shelter," Anora said.

"Yes," Nelda agreed. "This drizzle will soon become a driving rain."

"We better make for the next cave we see," Bret said. "There may be some around the bend up ahead where the trail cuts back against the mountains."

* * * * *

When Bret and the women rounded the curve they saw a glow coming from a little valley beside the road.

"That looks like a bonfire," Bret said.

"Yes," Anora agreed. "Do you suppose whoever built it would mind if we shared the warmth with them?"

"We could ask," Bret said. "All they can do is tell us to get lost."

In the gathering darkness of the coming storm Bret and his companions turned off the road and made for the small valley. As they moved toward the fire they heard the faint sound of voices. At first they were just a murmur, but as Bret and the women approached the valley they rose to a chant.

* * * * *

The travelers had just reached the cluster of boulders at the edge of the valley when thunder rolled and lightning flashed. Momentarily the valley was lit by a blue-white light, revealing a bizarre scene that stopped Bret and his friends in their tracks.

Black robed figures were dancing around the huge bonfire brandishing torches and chanting loudly. Atop a crude stone altar, next to the fire, lay a woman; her naked body covered with strange symbols. She writhed and moaned as a figure dressed in red stood over her, caressing her body and mouthing incantations.

"Who are they?" Anora asked.

"I'm afraid we've stumbled onto something we aren't supposed to see," Yolette said. "I've heard stories about a deadly coven of male witches that inhabit the caves and valleys hereabouts. They are led by the warlock Kairos. And next to the ruler of this evil land, he is the most feared person around.

"According to some, he was a powerful magician in Egypt during the time of the exodus. He was one of the Pharaoh's palace magicians that engaged Moses in the famous contest having to do with the staffs and cobras."

"It's agreed among the other wizards that he could easily win the reckoning every year," Nelda said. "But he feels it's beneath his dignity to engage in a contest with wizards he considers so inferior to himself."

"Kairos would like to rule here," Anora said. "But he hasn't the power to overthrow the one who lives in the castle within the lake of fire. He is favored by Satan and fully supported by him. No warlock can win over another who enjoys such protection."

"So Kairos must be content to rule in the shadowy places of the land, enjoying a certain amount of notoriety," Yolette said. "The coven he leads here has the single distinction of using a living altar, a young woman taken captive and drugged by a potion forced upon her. As a grand finale to the ceremony, Kairos will cut her heart out and throw it into the fire."

"We better haul ass out of here," Bret said. "We don't want to get mixed up with this gang."

As Bret turned to lead the women back to the trail two figures blocked their way. They were tall, dressed in black hooded robes, and carrying torches.

"You are intruders," one of them said. "Kairos will not suffer an unbeliever to witness our ceremony and live."

"You will pay with your life for your spying," the other said.

As they advanced Bret leaped forward, sinking his dagger to the hilt in one of the figure's stomach.

"Master!" he screamed, "intruders are watching!"

Bret jerked the knife out and sank it again, this time in the man's chest. He let out a shrill scream as the blade penetrated his heart, then sank to the ground dead. Nelda flashed forward and thrust the tip of her cutlass into the other man's chest. He stumbled back and collapsed.

Bret picked up one of the fallen torches. "Let's get out of here!" he shouted, "before the whole bunch comes down on us."

But the noise had attracted the attention of Kairos and his followers. They stopped their ceremony and formed into a group with Kairos at their head. Then with angry shouts he surged forward, his minions close behind him.

Bret and the women had a head start and made it to the road well ahead of their pursuers. Lightning flashed and thunder rolled as the storm hit in full fury. Rushing headlong into the pelting rain Bret desperately scanned the cliffs at the side of the road for any sign of a cavern. Then he saw one, barely visible through the driving rain.

"Over here!" he shouted. He ran toward the opening, the women following close behind. Just inside the mouth of the cave Bret and the women leaned against the wall of the tunnel to catch their breath. Cautiously Bret looked out.

"Damn," he said. "They must have seen us come in here. They're making straight for us."

Bret and his friends knew they had to either stand and fight or retreat farther into the mountain. Considering the odds against them, retreat seemed their only option.

* * * * *

At length the tunnel terminated in a large cavern. Bret held the torch high as he scanned the surroundings. Several large boulders sat imbedded in the circular wall around them, but there was no passage out.

Bret led the women to the opposite wall where they stood with their backs against it, awaiting the inevitable attack. Nelda drew her cutlass and stood staring at the opening of the tunnel, her jaw set in grim determination.

"Those bloody brigands won't have an easy time of it with me," she vowed.

Bret shoved the torch into the sandy floor, extinguishing it and plunging the group into total blackness. His heart pounding, he stood in the dark with his friends, barely daring to breathe, gripping the handle of the dagger.

* * * * *

A faint light emanated from the tunnel and Bret and his companions heard the sound of angry voices. The voices grew louder and the light brighter. Then, suddenly a group of black robed figures burst into the cavern. They stood with their torches held high, surveying the trapped party across the circular cave. Then Kairos pushed his way through the mob and stood against the wall. On his signal one of the dark figures stuck his torch in the dirt before his master and moved swiftly away.

His demonic features accentuated by the blazing torch, Kairos stood for a moment glaring at Bret and the women. Then he motioned to a figure at his side. The man drew a sword from under his black robe and advanced on the trapped party.

Nelda stepped forward to meet him and the cavern rang with the sound of clashing metal. Kairos had expected a quick victory for his servant, more of an execution than a fight. But Nelda proved to be more than a match for the warlock. At the outset he found himself fighting a loosing battle, barely able to fend off her attacks. It was a short conflict as Nelda quickly found an opening and slit her adversary's throat, nearly decapitating him.

Snarling Kairos sent two more men at Bret and the women. As they advanced Anora and Yolette pelted them with a hail of stones. Cursing, the figures retreated. His face livid with rage, Kairos ordered his minions out of the cavern.

"I don't think we licked them," Bret said. "I'm sure they'll be back."

"Probably," Nelda said. She swung the cutlass, making a swishing noise as it sliced through the air. "Damn," she said, "I'd forgotten what it felt like to use this." She smiled broadly. "It felt damned good," she said.

"You're pretty good with that thing," Bret said. "Where did you learn to use a sword like that?"

"This is not the time to get into it," Nelda said. "But it's quite a story."

"If we ever get out of here," Bret said, "I'd sure like to hear it."

Suddenly there was a rumbling outside the cavern as rocks and debris began falling from the roof of the tunnel. Bret and his companions flattened against the opposite wall as clouds of dust billowed into the cavern. When, at last, the rumbling stopped they peered through the dust at the rock and rubble blocking the only way out of the cavern.

CHAPTER 7

Bret and the women huddled against the cavern wall, the clouds of dust so thick they could hardly breathe. They coughed uncontrollably, their eyes burned, and they could barely see each other through the swirling brown mantle of dirt that filled the cavern.

When at last the dust settled Bret and the women walked across the cavern to the closed passage. For a moment they stood looking at the rocks and rubble clogging the exit. Finally Bret took a deep breath and shrugged his shoulders.

"Well," he said, "might as well get started." He reached out and tugged at a large rock.

"It's useless," Anora said. "We'll never get out of here."

"Maybe not," Bret replied. "But I'm not going to die here without at least trying to get out."

Nelda and Yolette came to his aid, and the three brought the rock tumbling to the floor of the cavern. Bret smiled and grabbed another, smaller rock, wrestling it from the passage. Anora joined the others and soon they had the rocks cleared a few feet into the tunnel. Then dirt and dust began falling from the ceiling.

"Get out of here!" Bret shouted. "It's going to cave-in again."

As he and his companions rushed back into the cavern the small inroad they had made in the tunnel was again filled with falling stones and dirt.

Now Bret realized that trying to clear the passage was useless, the cave-in reached too far back into the tunnel. And what was worse, they had used up precious air in their futile attempt to clear the rubble from the cave.

So what? Bret thought. Now they would die a few minutes sooner than if they had done nothing, in which case death would have been a certainty. At least they tried.

The torch was burning precious oxygen, but Bret and his companions didn't care. If they were to die of suffocation, they would rather it not be in darkness. And there was no need to prolong the inevitable.

As they sat against the wall Bret turned to Nelda at his side. "Since we don't appear to be going anywhere," he told her, "maybe this would be a good time to tell me about yourself."

Nelda turned to Bret, a look of unbelief on her face. "You want me to tell you about myself now?" she asked. Bret nodded. "Whatever for?" she questioned. "What difference could it make now?" She looked deeply into Bret's eyes, her own reflecting deep sorrow and helplessness. "You do realize, don't you," she went on, "we're all going to die? We may never meet again. So why would you want to know about me?"

"Now that's something I don't understand," Bret said.

"What?" Yolette asked.

"This whole dying thing."

"What don't you understand about it?"

"Well, with the exception of myself, hasn't everybody here died in one way or another?" Yolette nodded. "Then," Bret continued, "how can they die again?"

"Most here have died many times," Yolette told him.

Bret shook his head and put up his hands in a sign of surrender. "Wait a minute," he said. "You lost me. How can that be?"

"Remember I told you the physical world was only one part of reality?"

"Yes."

"Well, this place is the physical world to us that inhabit it. To us it is reality. And we can suffer the pain of dying. But it isn't true death, not release from suffering. It's just another form of torment we endure. We pass to another place in this same world. We may or may not be with the people we knew in our former existence but we retain all memory of it."

"How do you know that?" Bret asked.

Yolette shrugged. "We all know it," she said. "That's part of the torment to know we can never leave this place no matter how many times we die. We only go on to suffer on another plain."

"But you have physical bodies," Bret insisted. "Or is that just an illusion?"

Anora put her hand on Bret's shoulder. "It's no illusion," she assured him. "When anyone here suffers what passes for death," she went on, "within a few minutes their body follows their spirit to the next incarnation, whatever that may be."

Bret shook his head. "I don't know," he murmured, "that's pretty hard to believe."

"Then where is Kairos' follower, the one Nelda killed?" Anora asked.

"He's right over there, where he fell," Bret said pointing to the center of the cavern. His eyes widened in surprise. "But," he stammered, "he was there. Where did he go?"

"To join his spirit on the next plain in an endless cycle of torment," Yolette said.

Bret walked to the opposite wall and picked up the torch. Then he went to the center of the cavern and inspected the ground. There were signs of a scuffle where the warlock and Nelda had engaged in swordplay and an impression where he had fallen. The dirt was still stained by his blood but there was no sign of his body. Finally Bret stuck the torch in the dirt and turned to the women.

"He's gone all right," he said. He walked back to where the women sat against the wall. Slowly he sank to the ground next to Nelda. He picked up a handful of dirt and angrily threw it toward the center of the cavern. He heaved a sigh and put his hand on Nelda's arm. She turned to meet his gaze.

"So, if this is it," Bret said with a casual air, "why not satisfy my curiosity? Tell me how you came to be here."

"It really doesn't matter now," Nelda began, "It's like Yolette said . . . "

"I don't care about that," Bret insisted. "I'd still like to know."

"Go ahead," Anora encouraged Nelda.

"But you and Yolette already know the story."

"That's all right," Yolette said. "Anora and I don't mind hearing it again. And besides it'll help pass the time."

Nelda took a deep breath and exhaled slowly. "All right," she said, "I was born in Liverpool, England, in 1663. My father was a wealthy outfitter and a good fifteen years senior to my mother, Nora. I was the only child of one of the most affluent families in Liverpool, and, I'm afraid, pretty spoiled. I adored my father and he could refuse me nothing.

"He was a fencing enthusiast and taught me to use an epee when I was only six. My mother was not real keen on the idea of my father teaching me what she called barbaric skills. She thought I should be learning ladylike things. But since I enjoyed the time spent with my father so much, for the time being, she didn't actively oppose my training in what was admittedly a man's thing. By the age of ten I was well accomplished with fencing foils as well as the saber and cutlass.

"But as I began t grow out of childhood my mother felt I should discontinue the sport as it was unladylike. Reluctantly, my father was inclined to agree with her."

A look of sadness came to Nelda's eyes. She paused for a moment to wipe away a tear, then continued.

"My father died when I was only twelve years old," she went on. "When I was fifteen my mother remarried to Tucker Walcot, a local banker. He was a rich, lecherous old fart who thought everything was for sale. He made my skin crawl when I'd catch him leering at me. I told my mother how I felt about him, but she refused to believe he was that sort.

* * * * *

"When I was sixteen my Aunt in Manchester became gravely ill and my mother went to care for her. I dreaded seeing her go because she would be gone for a fortnight.

"My mother's carriage had scarcely left the driveway of our mansion when Tucker began on me. At first it was just verbal, remarking on my figure, telling me what a beautiful woman I was; that sort of twaddle. I told him I didn't like it but that didn't stop him. Then he began touching me whenever he came within arm's reach.

"By the end of the week I was staying mostly in my room to avoid his unwanted attention. Then on the eve of my mother's return my stepfather came home roaring drunk and kicked in the door to my bedroom. I wasn't strong enough to fight off his advances and he had his way with me.

"When he had finished and fell into a drunken sleep I went downstairs and curled up on the couch in the parlor. I couldn't sleep for fear he'd wake up and come downstairs and abuse me again. I huddled in sickening fright on the couch throughout the remainder of the night.

* * * * *

"My mother found me there when she arrived before dawn. She asked me why I was sleeping there instead of in my bed upstairs. I told her what had happened. I had never seen my mother angry. In most unladylike language I had never heard her use before, she vowed Tucker Walcot would pay for his crime. She would go to the police station to lodge a complaint as soon as it opened. But, with her usual sense of practicability, she felt we should have breakfast first.

* * * * *

"Mother and I were in the kitchen preparing breakfast for ourselves when Tucker Walcot walked in. He rushed to my mother but she rebuffed him. He asked what was the matter and she told him she would be going to the police about what had happened in the house the night before.

"Of course he denied the whole thing. And when it was apparent to him he would not convince my mother he went berserk, grabbing her by the throat. In a blind rage, I picked up a butcher knifed and drove it into his back.

"With his being well known and respected in all the financial circles my mother and I knew no one would believe us when we told them what happened. In the eyes of the law I would be found responsible for Tucker Walcot's death and my mother would be considered an accomplice.

* * * * *

"My mother went to a sea captain, an old friend of bygone days when my father fitted most all the ships in Liverpool harbor. He was to sail to the New World on the next tide within the hour. When my mother told him what had happened he offered to secretly take us along.

"There was no time to make a bank withdrawal so we took what cash was in the house, packed a few clothes, and returned to the ship just as they were weighing anchor. Within a few minutes the ship had cleared the harbor and headed west into the Irish Sea. Sixty knots out of Liverpool, just passing the Anglesey Peninsula aport, the ship turned south through St. George's Channel, into the Atlantic, and we were on our way to the New World.

* * * * *

"The ship was bound for Kingston on the island of Jamaica where it would offload its cargo of Irish linen and pick up one of rum. But we never made it to Kingston. We had just sighted the Bahamas dead ahead when the pirate ship appeared off our starboard bow.

"An attack was imminent and the captain sent us to his cabin. It would afford little protection but it was the best he could do. My mother put me in the clothespress while she hid under the bed.

* * * * *

"The pirate ship fired a shot across our bow. When the captain didn't heave to the buccaneer fired again, striking the captain's cabin. The entire stern of the ship above the waterline was blown away by the blast. In the sturdy oak closet, against the forward bulkhead of the cabin, my life was spared. But my mother, under the bed against the stern, was killed instantly.

"I stepped out of the clothespress and stumbled across the deck, my ears ringing. The stern bulkhead of the cabin had been blown away and the deck ended abruptly in a ragged mass of beams and planking. I looked out onto the expanse of ocean to see the pirate ship approaching. Quickly it closed, scraping alongside, entangling their rigging with ours. Then the filthy cutthroats swarmed over the gunnels of the trapped ship and slaughtered the crew to a man.

* * * * *

"I was discovered hiding in what was left of the captain's cabin. He had given me a pistol for protection. But it was of little use when the pirates burst into the cabin. I killed the one in the lead, but before I could reload the others took the pistol away from me and hustled me on deck.

* * * * *

"When I was taken before the pirate captain they made no mention of my shooting one of them. I suppose, to them, it meant one less to share the booty with.

"The leader of the pirate crew was Captain Thornton Huxford, referred to by his men as Captain Thorn. He leered at me standing helpless before him, his crew at my back.

"Well now," he said, "what have we here?"

"We found her hiding in the captain's cabin," one of the pirates said. "She's a fair wench, and untouched I'd say. Thought you'd want the first time with her."

"Mighty thoughtful of you," the captain sneered.

"What about the rest of us?" another buccaneer asked. "Do we get a chance at her?"

Captain Thorn grinned. "Of course," he said, "we all share with our shipmates."

* * * * *

"A hasty lottery was arranged. Under the captain's supervision several slips of paper were put into an empty rum cask. One slip had a black dot on it. The man who drew this would have first chance at me." Nelda paused, a look of disgust on her face. "I suppose," she went on, "Captain Thorn planned a similar lottery each day to pass me around equitably among the crew. But I put a quick stop to any such idea.

"When the man who drew the black dot started for me I backed up till I was stopped by the pirate behind me. They jeered and laughed as they blocked my way. But I had no intention of trying to break through their ranks. Where would I have gone? I was a prisoner on the ship.

"As the sneering freebooter closed on me I jerked a dagger from the belt of one of the pirates looking on. The sneering, slobbering brute kept coming, thinking I wouldn't have the nerve to use the knife. But he soon found out how wrong he was. His mouth flew open and his eyes widened in terror as I sank the knife into his belly. When I felt the blood gush out and run over my hand, he suddenly became the symbol of my life's pain, disappointment, and hatred. As he collapsed to the deck I went berserk, stabbing him repeatedly. The stunned crew looked on while I kept plunging the knife into his chest and belly. Then I rose to face the captain. Behind me the scurvy pirate crew murmured in disbelief.

"Well strike me pink," Captain Thorn said, an amused expression on his face. "We got a tiger on our hands me buckoes. She'd be the match of any man jack among you in a battle, I'll wager."

"More than a match for any of this scurvy lot," I screamed, the adrenaline still pumping through my veins. Captain Thorn laughed and jokingly asked if I would consider joining his crew. Although I knew he was toying with me I decided to treat the situation seriously. I told him that since I had no alternative I would join his company. But I warned him to keep his crew of filthy vermin away from me or he wouldn't have any crew. The smile left his lips and he glared at me. The crew behind me stood silent, awaiting the captain's wrath. Then Captain Thorn laughed again.

"By God," he roared, "I like your spirit." Then he spoke directly to the crew. "If any of you try and force your attentions on our newest member of the brotherhood you'll have me to answer to." Then with a grin, he added, "That is if you survive."

* * * * *

"Over the next few years the crew soon learned to respect me as an equal. When boarding a ship at sea, I was usually in the forefront of battle. My early training in the art of fencing served me well. But there was no place for the sportsmanship that went along with the sport. I soon learned to be merciless with my foes and expect no quarter from them. It was a philosophy that kept me alive.

* * * * *

"For five years I sailed with Captain Thorn, plundering merchant ships in the Caribbean. I never made any attempt to hide the fact that I was a woman, and soon became well known. Perhaps not as famous as Ann Bonny, but still well known in pirate circles.

* * * * *

"It was during a stopover in Port-au-Prince for provisions that I first met Aubury Guignard, the owner of a waterfront bar. He was the same man known to Yolette as Gano Guvier and Anora as Perrin Fortier.

"He enjoyed the reputation as quite the lady's man. It was said that any woman he went after he got. And, of course, me being somewhat of a celebrity, he wanted to add my scalp to his belt.

* * * * *

The night he killed me we were sitting at a table in a dark corner of his bar. I'll admit he was a handsome fellow. And had he played his cards right we would have become lovers. But I was too used to my independence and resented his attitude of superiority. When I told him so he slapped me.

"My first instinct was to slit his throat. But he was a powerful man in Port-au-Prince and I didn't want to alienate his friends. I knew that from time to time we would need his services, as every freebooter did. We couldn't stay at sea forever, and had to come into port sometime to deal with them.

"So, instead of drawing my blade, I threw my tankard of ale in his face and started to leave. He grabbed my arm and began to twist it, telling me I'd do whatever he ordered.

"My anger flared up and I no longer cared what his friends thought, I wanted to kill him. I managed to get my dagger out with my other hand and stab him in the shoulder. He didn't seem to feel any pain, it only made him angrier. He tightened his grip on my arm until I thought he'd crush the bone. All the time he seemed unconcerned about the dagger buried to the hilt in his shoulder.

"I was so shocked all I could do was look at him. He snarled then grabbed me by the hair with one hand and jerked the dagger from his shoulder with the other. Then he pulled me across the table, forcing my face down against its top. He had unbelievable strength, like maybe twenty men. I was completely helpless as he forced my face down on the tabletop. I called out for help from my shipmates who were in the bar. But my pleas were drowned out by the crowd noises.

"Then I felt the pain as he stabbed me in the back with my own dagger. Then everything went black when he plunged the blade into the back of my neck at the base of my skull.

"Soon I was again aware of what was happening. But I was unable to move, to do anything, like I was watching a scene from a detached position. He covered me with his coat until it was almost dawn and the place closed. Then he carried me to the bar and lay me down on it. He spouted some mumbo-jumbo and waved his hands. I felt like my body was rising and moving toward the mirror. When I reached it my body seemed to become fluid and I passed right through it.

"The next thing I knew I was here in this accursed place. For a time I could look through the mirror onto the world I had left. But one night a few years after I was sent here the mirror was broken in a bar brawl."

Nelda sighed and looked at the flickering, dying torch across the cavern.

"It's about to go out," she said. "We've used up all the air in here."

"Guess we better conserve what's left," Bret suggested. "Don't move and don't talk."

"Why so?" Nelda asked. "If we're going to die why prolong it?"

"If I don't meet you all on the next plain," Yolette said, "I want you to know I'll miss your friendship."

"And I yours," Anora told her.

The group fell silent, staring into the gathering darkness.

* * * * *

Bret and the women were now gasping for breath. The oxygen in the cavern was nearly exhausted. Then, in the last rays of the dying torch he thought he saw one of the boulders imbedded in the cavern wall move. He peered intently into the growing darkness and heard a scraping sound. The boulder was moving, sliding to the side. Then light spilled from an opening behind it.

As Bret and the women watched, still weak from their near suffocation, two figures emerged from the opening holding torches high above their heads.

For an instant they stood curiously eyeing the four across the cavern, then started toward them. Bret tried to struggle to his feet, but was still too weak to manage it.

"Looks like we aren't going to die after all," Nelda said in a feeble voice.

"Maybe not," Anora said. "Or maybe we will, but in some different way."

Breathing deeply, trying to regain his strength, Bret watched the figures cross the cavern toward them.

CHAPTER 8

The man that led the small group into the cavern was tall and gaunt. His drooping black mustache leaped intro prominence against the gray pallor of his furrowed face. His eyes, sunken deep in their sockets, were set in a cold hypnotic stare.

Like his companions, he wore a tattered brown wool uniform, its brass buttons tarnished, his boots scuffed and unpolished. The patent leather bill of his garrison cap was peeling, the once shiny brass insignia corroded. His mustache and the master sergeant's chevrons on his sleeve were all that distinguished him from his similarly dressed, cleanshaven companions.

The sergeant walked cautiously to where Bret lay on the ground. His deep set, pale blue eyes were like the eyes of a dead man, betraying no emotion as he stared down at Bret and the women. Then with a grunt he slung the bolt action rifle he carried on his shoulder and turned to his companions.

"All right, lads," he said, "help these civilians to their feet. Let's get them back to headquarters."

"Right you are, sarge," one of the men said as he helped Bret to his feet. Then casting an appreciative glance at the women, he commented, "I wouldn't mind a permanent detail of tending those three."

"Knock that off, trooper," the sergeant snapped. "We got more important things to worry about now than a bit of quiff." He pointed to the collapsed tunnel. "We'll not go to the outside on our foraging missions through there anymore," he said. "And you know what that means."

"Through the other passage," the man said with an unmistakable tone of fear in his voice. "But what about the . . . "

"We'll discuss that at a more appropriate time," the sergeant interrupted. Then, turning to Bret, he asked, "Are you and your lady friends up to a short march?"

"Sure," Bret replied. "But who are you?" He waved his arm in the direction of the others. "And who are they? Where did you come from?"

The sergeant regarded Bret with the look of mild contempt he reserved for someone he considered soft but capable of being toughened into a real man.

"For someone who just came within a gnat's ass of dying," he growled, "you sure ask a lot of questions."

"One of the traits of my occupation," Bret replied.

"And what would that be?"

"I'm a writer."

The sergeant wrinkled his nose as though smelling an unpleasant odor.

"Well," he sneered, "I suppose someone has to be. But I've always thought that's a job better suited to women." Bret bristled but made no reply. "Seems to me like a sissy way for a grown man to make a living," the sergeant went on. "But that's just me. I'm sure there are those that would disagree."

"Almost any educated person would," Bret snapped back. The sergeant smiled at Bret's anger and hooked his thumb under the sling of his rifle, readjusting its weight on his shoulder. "Throw down that rifle and tell your men to stay out of it," Bret invited, "and we'll see how much of a sissy I am."

The sergeant smiled broadly, turned to his men, nodded knowingly, and again faced Bret.

"Well now," he said, "looks like I may have misjudged you. I can see we're going to get along swimmingly."

"O.K.," Bret said, his sudden flare of anger subsiding, "so we're going to be buddies. Then how about answering my question."

"Later. Right now we have to fall back to our headquarters to plan a new strategy." The sergeant turned and walked across the cavern toward the opening in the wall. "Well, come on," he growled over his shoulder. "Or do you plan to spend the rest of your time in this bloody cavern?"

* * * * *

Bret and the women entered the passage behind the sergeant and the others followed. The last man through the portal pulled a lever on the wall and the boulder slid sideways, closing the passage.

"Pretty clever," Bret commented. "How did you discover that?"

"We didn't discover it," the sergeant snorted, "we built it."

"How does it work?"

"The boulder is set on small rollers that run on a hidden slide below the surface of the floor. Counterweights make it possible to move the heavy rock with little effort." The sergeant shrugged his shoulders. "It's a crude setup," he said, "but it works."

"It must have taken a long time to rig that up," Bret observed.

The sergeant grinned. "Well," he said, "time is what we got the most of here."

* * * * *

The ragtag group led Bret and his companions through a series of tunnels into a circular, high domed cavern. Through small openings in the ceiling a dim, eerie light fell on the floor. Water from the rainstorm outside formed small pools on the floor as it dripped from the stalactites clinging to the ceiling.

Away from the center of the cavern a line of pup tents stretched along one wall in an orderly fashion. At one end of the row stood a rock cubicle some ten feet square with a roof made from the canvas of several pup tents laced together. Over the doorway, curtained off by a tattered blanket, was a crudely lettered sign reading "Headquarters, 1st Battalion – 4th Norfork Regiment."

* * * * *

The sergeant stopped in front of the cubicle and dismissed his men. As they walked away he turned to Bret and the women.

"Battalion Sergeant Major Carney, of the New Zealand Volunteers, at your service," he said, touching the bill of his cap in a salute.

Bret shook the sergeant's outstretched hand and introduced himself and the women.

"Your unit sounds vaguely familiar," he told the sergeant. "I'm sure I've heard something about it. But can't recall where."

"Ah," Sergeant Carney said with a proud smile, "so you've heard of us." He stood a little more erect and threw out his chest. "Well," he went on, "if I do say so myself, the men of the First Battalion always gave a good account of themselves in every campaign they were a part of."

"Of course," Bret beamed, "I remember now. You're the famous Lost Battalion of World War One."

Sergeant Carney's face took on a sad look. "I suppose people do remember us that way," he lamented.

Bret looked around. "Are there more of you somewhere?" he asked.

"Just what you see, buddy," Sergeant Carney replied.

"Well you look to be several men short of a battalion," Bret quipped. "I don't see more than a dozen at best."

"We've suffered casualties over the years."

"You mean in the real world or after you got here?"

"Both. We weren't up to authorized strength that day at Gallipoli. But things weren't going well for our lads so we had to lend a hand."

"What happened?" Bret asked.

Sergeant Carney smiled proudly. "Ah," he began, "now that's quite a yarn. One you'll probably be inclined to doubt."

"Around here," Bret declared, "I'd believe anything. Tell me what happened."

Sergeant Carney motioned toward the doorway to the stone cubicle. "Come on in to the orderly room," he said. "And I'll tell you all about it."

* * * * *

Bret and the women followed the sergeant into the cubicle. Against one wall sat a crudely constructed desk and a small barrel that served as a chair. There were four additional barrels in front of the desk. A narrow shelf ran the length of the opposite wall. Above this hung a map, sketched in charcoal on a piece of canvas. An oil lamp sitting on the corner of the desk dimly lit the room.

Sergeant Carney sat behind the desk and waved the others to the barrels. When they were seated he leaned back against the wall, twirling his mustache.

"It was the 21st of August, in the year 1915 at Gallipoli," he began. "In case you didn't know, that's a Turkish peninsula that forms the northwest shore of the Dardanelles," he explained. Bret and the women nodded. "The British Tommys and us colonial lads from New Zealand were giving the Turks what for," Carney went on. "But things took a turn for the worse when the battle lines reached a hilly area. The Turks had taken the high ground, putting our lads at a considerable disadvantage. Orders came down for our unit to take a position designated Hill 40.

"It was a breezy day, but, oddly, the clouds didn't move in the sky. They just hung there, as though frozen in time. We were advancing toward hill 40 and one cloud in particular, in front of us, looked more dense than the others, almost like a solid structure resting on the ground near the hill.

"The 1st Battalion – 4th Norfork Regiment marched up a dry creek toward hill 40, directly into the cloud. When we first entered the mist if felt cool and refreshing. Then, all around, it took on a glare of light that almost blinded us.

"Suddenly I found myself atop a hill in this Godforsaken place, with several of my comrades. At first I thought we were still in Gallipoli, separated from the rest of the unit. When I looked down the hill it was like looking through a tunnel of light. I could see quite clearly directly in front of me, but things became distorted and dark at the periphery."

Sergeant Carney paused to look at Bret and the women. Satisfied he had their undivided attention; he went on.

"At the base of the hill I could see my comrades in arms still marching into the cloud. But no one ever came out the other side. After the last file had disappeared into it the cloud lifted off the ground and slowly rose to join others. Then the whole mass moved away to the west

"I don't know what happened to the rest of the battalion. I suppose they're somewhere in this hellish place. But I don't know where.

"At first I tried to keep my men in the open. But I soon learned it was much safer inside the caverns."

"Quite a story," Bret said. "And, as I told you, in this place, I believe every word of it."

"Thank you," Sergeant Carney said. "I appreciate that. But now we have more pressing things to discuss." He rose, picked up the oil lamp from the desk, and walked to the map. He sat the light on the shelf, studied the crude chart for a moment, then turned to the others. "This," he began, "is a map of the surrounding area. It's the result of exhaustive reconnaissance and I believe it to be fairly accurate. You'll notice the whole place is honeycombed with caves. Many are dead ends but some connect to large caverns." He pointed to a section in the center of the map. "We're here," he said. "Previously, on our foraging patrols we went through this tunnel, to the large cavern here." His finger rested on the site where Bret and the women had nearly suffocated. "Then," he continued, tracing a route with his finger, "we'd go through this tunnel, connecting with this one leading to the outside."

Sergeant Carney paused for a moment, turned to face Bret and the women, then went on.

"As we all know," he said, "that tunnel is now blocked by a cave-in." The sergeant slapped the crude map with the palm of his hand. "We've tried to find alternate routes to the outside," he said, "if for no other reason than retreat, should it become necessary. But all the other tunnels we've been able to explore are blocked by cave-ins. We tried to clear them but the roofs keep crumbling. So we finally gave up. I'm afraid the main tunnel off the cavern where we found you may be the same."

"It is," Bret told him. "We tried to dig our way out of the cavern but the tunnel kept collapsing."

"How did you come to be in the cavern anyway?" Carney asked. "Most here stay on the surface."

"We were being chased by a coven of witches. We stumbled on to their ceremony. They caught us watching and didn't take too kindly to that. They came at us and in the skirmish we killed two of their number.

"Since we were outnumbered we took to the caves to try and shake them. But they finally got us trapped in the cavern where you found us. We didn't know there was another way out. When the witches tried to take us Nelda separated one of them from his head with her cutlass."

Sergeant Carney cast an admiring glance at Nelda. "Well," he said with a broad smile, "a warrior as well as a fine looking lass." He studied the group for an instant, his eyebrows knitted in thought. "Do you have any idea who it was that chased you into the cavern?" he asked.

"We're pretty sure it was Kairos and his coven," Yolette said.

"Damn," Sergeant Carney said. "I was afraid of that. We had only been here about a week when we had our run-in with that devil.

"We were bivouacked when we heard the noise and saw the torchlight. When we went to investigate they saw us. At the time I had eighteen troopers and we still had ammunition for our rifles. So I ordered them to stand and fight."

Sergeant Carney shook his head. "I still don't understand what happened," he said. "Our bullets didn't have any effect on the witches. They just kept coming. Five of my men were killed in hand-to-hand combat before we made our way into a cave at the side of the road. For some reason that I'll never know, they didn't follow us.

"Since then we've been living here, going out at night to forage for food and appropriate other supplies such as lumber from deserted dwellings, lamp oil, and the like. But now the tunnel to the outside is blocked and I doubt that we can ever clear it."

Bret studied the map. "There has to be another tunnel leading to the outside," he said. "Maybe you just haven't found it yet."

Sergeant Carney shook his head. "When you've been underground as long as we have," he said, "you'll know it isn't that simple. Some of these tunnels may connect with the outside. But they're impassible."

"Why?" Nelda asked.

"Some of them are swarming with giant bats," Carney replied. "We call them ghost bats because they're some sort of albino strain, white as snow. They're a bloodthirsty lot with a wingspan of over three feet and razor-sharp teeth that can rip the flesh right off your bones. Other passages are infested with scorpions and snakes. And I can tell you that's the best of it."

Sergeant Carney pointed to the map. "This cavern here," he said, "and the tunnels connecting it are inhabited by a most disagreeable bunch of creatures we call Trogs. They're a hairy, squat, snaggletooth bunch with round, staring eyes. And they stink to high heaven to boot.

"We ran onto them one day while scouting the area. They jumped us from ambush and we spent the last of our rifle ammunition on them with no effect whatsoever. It was just like the witches. I lost two men before we could disengage. Thankfully the Trogs didn't follow us. Apparently they're very territorial, but won't follow an enemy once they leave the area. Since that encounter we've always left them alone and they've done the same to us."

"How many would you say there were?" Bret asked.

"Hard to tell. It was pretty dark. But I'd guess about 25 or 30. Why do you ask?"

"We may have to fight our way through them to get out of these caves," Bret said.

"Weren't you listening" Sergeant Carney snapped. "I told you we couldn't kill the buggers. Our bullets had no effect on them."

"And it was the same with the witches, wasn't it?" Bret asked. Carney nodded. "But steel does have an effect on them," Bret declared. "I know that for a fact. Probably because it contains iron, a very powerful weapon against witches. I killed one of them with my dagger and Nelda killed one with her cutlass."

Sergeant Carney grinned. "Well now," he said, "that puts a completely different complexion on things." He jerked the bayonet from its scabbard on his hip and walked to where his rifle leaned against the wall. Picking up the weapon he fitted the blade to its muzzle. "The lads will like this," he beamed. "We haven't ran a bayonet charge in quite a while now."

CHAPTER 9

The men of the First Battalion stood at attention, their rifles slung over their shoulders. Slowly, Sergeant Carney walked the length of the rank and back again, scanning the faces of his troops. Then he took a position front and center.

"At ease," he growled in his usual rough manner. There was a shuffling of feet as the men relaxed. For a brief moment Sergeant Carney stared off into space, then clasped his hands behind his back and thrust out his chest in a gesture quite familiar to his men. It was the stance he took when about to deliver bad news. "Men," he began, "our usual route to the outside is no longer usable. We have to find another one." Casually he looked up toward the roof of the cavern as if in deep thought and stroked his mustache with the forefinger of his right hand. Then, slowly, he returned to his original stance. "That," he said, "means exploring other caves." There was a shuffling of feet and the exchange of anxious glances among Sergeant Carney's troops. "Today," he went on, sweeping his arm in the direction of the far wall of the cavern, "we'll have a go at the larger of the tunnels over there."

Sergeant Carney turned and walked the length of the rank and back, a grim expression on his face. It was another of his looks his men knew well. It was the one he wore when about to lead them into battle.

Again at his position of front and center, he turned to his troops. "There's a good possibility we'll come in contact with the Trogs again," he continued. "And you know what happened the last time we engaged them." A slight murmur rose from the men as they looked uneasily at each other. "But this time it'll be different," Sergeant Carney assured them. He turned to look at Bret and the women standing beside the orderly room and smiled. "Our new friends know a bit about these buggers," he went on. "And they assure me that even though bullets have no affect on them, these will."

With a dramatic flourish Sergeant Carney jerked his bayonet from its scabbard and held it aloft. Then, in a deep tone he snarled, "Fix bayonets."

* * * * *

The tunnel was just wide enough for three people to walk abreast. Sergeant Carney and Bret led the way with Anora, Nelda, and Yolette behind them, while the rest of the battalion followed. The torches, dispersed at short intervals along the column, spread a yellow glow that moved with it, leaving the area ahead and behind in total blackness.

* * * * *

As the party advanced the damp ground underfoot gave off the musty odor of a freshly turned grave. Just beyond the torchlight, in the blackness at the side of the tunnel, there could be heard the rustle of feet and scratching of claws on rocks. Occasionally Bret and his companions caught a glimpse of shadowy, baleful creatures, their beady eyes glinting in the torchlight as they scurried away.

Anora moved to Bret's side and slipped her arm around his waist. Feeling the slight shudder of her body he put his arm around her shoulder and drew her close.

"Don't worry," he assured her in a soft voice, "we'll make it out of here."

She lay her head on his shoulder. "I know," she said in a quavering voice that in spite of her best efforts betrayed grave doubt.

Bret moved his arm down around her waist. "Trust me," he said.

"I do," Anora told him. Then she put her lips close to Bret's ear. "But on the off chance we don't," she whispered softly, "I want you to know something." Bret nodded but made no reply. "If," Anora continued in a halting voice, "we are able to destroy the evil one's book of shadows . . ."

"What do you mean *if?*" Bret interrupted. "There's no if about it. You mean *when* we destroy it."

Anora nodded. "When we destroy the book," she began again, "this world we now know will probably cease to exist. We'll all be in a different, and I hope, a better place. Maybe Nelda, Yolette, and I will be together, maybe not. But since you didn't die in your past life as we did, I'm pretty sure you and I won't end up on the same plain. So I just wanted to say I'm glad it was you that found my portrait and are now sharing these last days here with me."

Bret tightened his grip around her waist. "I wouldn't have missed it for the world," he whispered.

* * * * *

Sergeant Carney halted the column as they reached a spur cave leading off at a sharp angle.

"Any ideas as to which way?" he asked Bret.

"I think it would be better to stick to the larger main tunnel," he replied. "It's been going pretty much in a straight line."

"Yes," Carney agreed. "But has it been going toward the outside, or deeper into the mountain?"

Bret shook his head. "Your guess is as good as mine," he said.

"We follow the main tunnel," the sergeant declared. "It's a 50-50 chance of getting outside."

Bret smiled. "How do you figure those odds?" he asked.

Sergeant Carney shrugged his shoulders. "Either we will or we won't," he said. "Either way we've given it a bloody go."

* * * * *

As the tunnel made a slight bend it opened into a small grotto. In the dim light of the torches, another tunnel could be seen leading out of the cavern across the way. A rock shelf, halfway up the wall, ran the length of one side of the cavern. Against the opposite wall lay a pool of inky-black water, fed by a trickle from a cleft in the cavern wall. There was a damp chill in the air and a blanket of mist hung over the dark pool like tiny wisps of ground fog.

Sergeant Carney led the way across the cavern to the mouth of the tunnel leading out and held up his hand.

"We'll have a bit of a rest here," he said. "But, mind you now, don't get too comfortable. We'll be moving out shortly."

Bret, Anora, Nelda, and Yolette sat and leaned against the rough rock wall. Nelda turned to look at Sergeant Carney setting next to her, twirling his mustache.

"You sure do like that cookie duster, don't you?" she asked.

Carney turned to her and smiled. "Yes, ma'am," he replied. "In a way, it's as much a symbol of my rank as these chevrons on my sleeve."

"How so?" Nelda asked, flashing an impish grin.

"Well, you see, in this man's army no one below the rank of sergeant is authorized a mustache. It isn't mandatory for sergeants, of course, but most men grow one when they attain the rank." Carney twirled his mustache and smiled. "Another privilege of the rank," he said, "is that you can marry." He paused a moment, then, as an afterthought, added, "But as far as that's concerned, well there are those that say if the army had wanted you to have a wife they'd have issued you one."

Nelda smiled and leaned closer to Carney. "And," she began in a mock conspiratorial voice, "I suppose they'd all look and perform the same. You know, like your rifles and other equipment."

"Well, miss, I never really gave that detail much thought. I certainly would hope not. That would take the fun of discovery out of things, now wouldn't it?"

Nelda flashed a flirtatious smile and lay her hand on Sergeant Carney's arm.

"Exactly my thinking," she said with a sultry smile. "I like men who think along the same lines I do." Tenderly she ran her hand the length of his sleeve, halting at the chevrons to trace their outline with her finger. "And, " Nelda said, still caressing the stripes on his sleeve, "I like men of authority."

Carney grinned broadly but before he could respond to Nelda's overture Anora sat upright and sniffed the air.

"Do you smell a strange odor?" she asked. "A sort of musty, sickening smell?"

Yolette took a deep breath and exhaled slowly. "Yes," she said, "now that you mention it, I do smell something strange. A sort of rotten vinegary odor."

Nelda got to her feet and looked in the direction of the stone shelf along one wall of the cavern.

"I hear a strange rustling sound coming from that wall, up there," she said. "Does anyone else hear it?"

"Yes, I do," Bret said. "It's getting louder." He looked intently at the stone ledge. "Did you see that?" he asked. "Something is dropping from the ledge. Whatever it is shines in the torchlight."

"It looks like rain," Nelda said, "except it's too big for raindrops.

Bret got to his feet and walked toward the wall, holding his torch high overhead. He had reached the center of the cavern when he whirled to face the others.

"It's scorpions," he shouted. "They're crawling down the wall and falling from the ledge. And they're the biggest ones I've ever seen. Some of those devils are a foot long if they're an inch. The floor over there is covered with them."

Sergeant Carney jumped to his feet. "The buggers are crawling out of the rocks up there," he said. "And they're moving toward the water like they were drawn to it somehow."

"Let's get out of here," Nelda said. "The smell of those bloody buggers is enough to make you sick to your stomach. I sure don't want to give them the chance to sink their stingers into me."

* * * * *

The cave leading out of the grotto was narrow and the party could walk no more than two abreast. At one point the roof was so low they were forced to crawl on their hands and knees, pushing the torches before them.

As they inched along in the close confines the heat and smoke burned their eyes and tortured their lungs. Ordinarily, they would have abandoned the burrow and retreated to the grotto to find another, more passable route. But Bret and his companions knew by now the floor to the grotto would be crawling with deadly scorpions and they had no choice but to press on.

A few torturous yards ahead the cramped burrow became a large tunnel. Relief washed over the travelers like a comforting tide and they trudged forward with renewed energy. They had gone only a few hundred yards when in the flickering light of their torches they could see the tunnel had widened into a long, deep gallery.

The trail leading through the stone corridor was flanked, on either side, by tall jagged rocks and short, stubby stalagmites jutting from the floor. The walls bore deep fractures running from floor to ceiling. Near the top of the gallery several ragged holes looked out over the trail below.

"I don't like this worth a damn," Sergeant Carney said. "The hair on the back of my neck is standing at attention. I can't shake the feeling that someone or something is watching us."

"I know what you mean," Bret said. "I have a bad feeling about this place too." He glanced at the ragged rocks at the side of the trail. "There's too many places for someone to hide," he said. "When we were in the narrow tunnel we weren't likely to be taken by surprise."

"I agree and suggest we get the hell out of here as fast as we can."

Bret and his friends looked up when they heard the sudden high-pitched screeches and the flapping noise from above. In the pale light of the torches they saw several white bats swooping down toward them.

Sergeant Carney and his men unslung their rifles and stood ready to skewer the albinos with their fixed bayonets. But as they neared Bret and his friends the strange flying mammals began to hover, the flapping sound of their giant wings and high-pitched screeches filling the air. Then, slowly, they began flying in an ever-narrowing circle. In the torchlight their beady pink eyes and sharp teeth flashing as they swooped nearer. Then one broke from the others and darted toward Yolette.

As the ghost bat swooped toward her its wing brushed the talisman around her neck. Instantly it fell to the floor screaming and flapping its wings in its death throes. The others swiftly flew upward and disappeared through the ragged openings of the passage at the top of the gallery.

"Blimey," Sergeant Carney said, "what scared them away?"

"I think it was my talisman," Yolette said. "The ghost bats are obviously another instrument of torment created by the evil one who rules this land. But the power of evil could not prevail over my amulet of hollow stone and iron."

"Before I got here," Sergeant Carney said, " I never put much stock in witches, magic, and such. But if you say it was your talisman that did the bat in I'll not disagree." Carney glanced up at the ceiling. "But all the same," he added, "we better get out of here before those buggers decide to have another go at us."

As the group started forward a Trog stepped from behind a rock ahead. Then two more appeared at the left of the trail. Turning, Bret saw the path behind blocked by the strange hairy creatures.

Sergeant Carney looked up at the sound of grunting. Dozens of Trogs clung to the jagged rocks at the side of the trail. Issuing unintelligible grunts and guttural sounds they slowly began descending, their huge, staring eyes riveted on the party below.

"Stand easy, lads," Sergeant Carney said. "We're outnumbered by quite a bit. Wait for my order. If they don't attack maybe we can ease our way by them without any trouble."

Slowly the first Trog to appear made his way toward Bret and his companions. As he stood in the torchlight he blinked several times then a dark membrane slowly moved from the outside corner of his bulging eyes to cover them.

"See that?" Bret asked, turning to Sergeant Carney.

"Yes, I did. I guess the blokes have lived in these dark caves so long they've developed another eyelid to protect their eyes from the light."

"Yes," Bret agreed. "A camel's eye works the same way to protect it from blowing sand."

Sergeant Carney looked suspiciously at the Trog. "I'm told snakes can do the same thing," he said.

The Trog walked slowly, reverently toward Yolette. Kneeling before her he picked up her foot and placed it on the back of his head in a sign of his servitude.

"What's happening," Sergeant Carney wanted to know.

"I'm not sure," Bret admitted, "but I think they saw what happened with the white bat and consider her some sort of god now."

More of the Trogs approached and soon the small party were surrounded by the hairy creatures. The one in front of Yolette rose, took her by the hand, and tugged gently.

"I think he wants me to follow him," she said.

"That would be my guess," Bret agreed. "I doubt very seriously they intend us harm. If they'd wanted to hurt us they could have done it already."

Sergeant Carney turned to his troops. "All right, men," he said, "we're going to follow these hairy blokes. They don't seem to be hostile at the moment, but keep alert and ready for anything."

Gently the Trog led Yolette through a gap in the wall of the gallery. Bret, Anora, and Nelda followed closely with their torches. Together they stepped through the opening into the passage. Sergeant Carney and his men followed. As the last of the troops disappeared into the tunnel the rest of the Trogs moved cautiously to the opening and trotted after them. Now Bret and his friends were confined in a tunnel, led by a strange creature to an unknown destination, with no chance of retreat.

CHAPTER 10

The tunnel was musty and damp, but the farther Bret and his companions followed the Trogs the fresher the air became. The torches began to flame higher with less smoke, casting more light on the surroundings.

* * * * *

When the group rounded a bend in the cavern they discovered it was no longer composed of natural rock. The tunnel was now a semicircular arch, its walls and ceiling formed of a white ceramic material having no discernible seams or joints. In stark contrast, the floor was covered with deep blue translucent tile. Wrought-iron sconces attached to the wall at intervals held burning torches, their flickering light bathing the white walls in a soft yellow glow.

* * * * *

Soon the party came to a door made of heavy wooden planks bound by wide wrought-iron straps held in place with large metal rivets. Three massive hinges held the door in its hewn rock casing. Light streamed through a small barred window near the top of the crude portal.
The Trog moved close to the door and tapped lightly, then issued a mournful moan. On the other side of the door a face appeared at the barred window, then the portal swung open. As the light poured through the open door the Trogs turned away from it and growled softly.

* * * * *

Beyond the door was a long corridor of a gray smooth material. A soft light emanated from recessed panels in the ceiling but cast no shadows.

The man standing on the other side of the door was squat and wiry. His long, shiny straight black hair fell to his shoulders, framing his ashen face and deep-set black eyes. His bright red, one-piece suit was cinched at the waist with a wide belt of a metallic material. On his right hip a holster hung from the belt, the handle of the pistol within easy reach of his hand. Around his neck he wore a silver colored medallion with a glowing egg-shaped stone set in the center. The tiara he wore was of the same metal, set with a smaller stone.

Along the corridor other men, similarly dressed, stood at close intervals, obviously guarding the passage. But unlike the man blocking the doorway they wore no tiaras. Instead their heads were covered with shiny metal helmets with massive nose guards that hid most of their faces. Also, the medallions around their necks were of smooth metal, containing no stones.

The man standing before Bret and his companions silently looked at them for a long moment, his black, unblinking eyes betraying no emotion. Then he glanced at the Trog standing nearby, his back still to the light. The man took a deep breath, pursed his lips, and let out a low whistle of varying musical pitch. The hairy creature responded with a long moan and lumbered away back up the tunnel, the others following. The man watched the Trogs disappear into the shadows then turned to Bret and his companions.

"You will follow me," he said curtly. "Lord Vidor is expecting you."

Carney stepped forward. "Sergeant Carney of the 1st Battalion, 5th Norfork Regiment," he proudly announced with a smart salute. The man looked at Carney with confusion. "My compliments to his lordship," the sergeant continued. "Please inform him that we are searching for a way to the outside and request leave to pass through his region."

The man looked at Sergeant Carney, for the first time his black eyes showing emotion. He was clearly confused and angered.

"I'm not your messenger," he growled. "I'm Sobola, aide-de-camp and chief counsel to Lord Vidor. I've been dispatched to bring you to him. Whatever case you may have you'll get the opportunity to argue it yourself." Haughtily, Sobola tuned and motioned to the two guards nearest him in the hallway. They walked quickly to his side and stood regarding Bret and his friends with icy stares, their hands on the butts of their pistols. "You will come with us," Sobola ordered. "Lord Vidor doesn't like to be kept waiting. Especially by those beneath him."

Bret and Sergeant Carney exchangedglances. "May as well go along with it for now," Bret suggested. "I think these guys mean business. And no telling how many of them there are."

Sergeant Carney nodded. "No way we could defend ourselves with bayonets against side arms in these close quarters," he said. "If we do have to take these blokes on I'd just as soon it be later, preferably somewhere with a little more maneuvering room." He turned to his men. "All right, lads," he said, "apparently, we've been invited in. So follow along single file. Mind your manners now and keep alert."

* * * * *

As Sobola led his prisoners along the corridor the guards stationed along the way stared curiously at them as they passed, paying special attention to the women.

Sergeant Carney glanced at Bret. "These blokes are really giving us the once-over," he said. "They're staring at us like we were in a bloomin' circus."

"Yeah," Bret agreed. "I think it's the way we're dressed, especially you and your men."

"What makes you think that?"

"These men are all dressed alike, so they must be members of some sort of military unit. But I've never seen uniforms like theirs before. Maybe the same goes for them. It's only natural they'd be just as curious about your uniforms as we are about theirs."

"Maybe so. But I think they're more interested in the women than what we're wearing." Carney grinned. "I haven't the foggiest where these blokes hail from," he said. "But they are men, that's a fact. And I'll wager like any bunch of troops assigned to a remote post, they're bored out of their minds and hornier than a mink in heat."

Bret nodded and smiled at Sergeant Carney's colorful simile. "You're probably right," he agreed. "Of course, not having the benefit of your obvious experience in such matters, I wouldn't know and, therefore, defer to your expert judgement."

"Yes, I've probably had more than my share of remote assignments. And, believe me, the nights get long and the days monotonous." Sergeant Carney shrugged his shoulders. "But it all counts for twenty," he said.

"Twenty?" Bret repeated questioningly.

"Yes, twenty. You know, twenty years. The magic number. Retirement." Bret nodded his understanding. "But," Carney went on in a doleful voice, "I suppose it doesn't matter much here." The sergeant cast a quick glance over his shoulder at his troops. "All right now, lads," he bellowed, "let's show these blokes how the First Battalion conducts themselves. Step out smartly now."

Sergeant Carney and his troops marched proudly forward, their eyes straight ahead, their heads held high. Although Anora and Yolette had no trouble keeping abreast of the pace they walked with their eyes downcast, their shoulders slumped in a submissive attitude. Nelda, on the other hand, moved along with a spring in her step, walking erect; her breast thrust proudly forward, and flashing a seductive smile at each guard as she passed. Their reaction ranged from surprise to broad smiles, befuddled grins, and lecherous leers.

Bret turned to Nelda and grinned. "Making a few new friends?" he asked.

"Right you are, love," she replied. "I learned long ago in my, to put it in the best possible terms, *seafaring* days, it's far better for a girl to be among friends than strangers."

"You have a good point. But let's hope whoever this Lord Vidor is he'll be friendly to us all."

"I wonder where he's from?" Nelda asked. "His men are oddly dressed. And they seem to have some power over those poor hairy devils in the caves."

"I'm sure you've noticed," Bret said, "that this cavern is man-made."

"Yes. The walls are too smooth to be natural. And the material is strange. Not like any plaster I've ever seen."

* * * * *

At length the strangely dressed escort brought Bret and the others to what appeared to be a dead-end in the tunnel. Sobola touched the stone in the medallion around his neck. Instantly there was a soft whirring noise and an opening appeared in the wall. Bret and his friends stood in silent awe as one instant the wall was solid, the next a passage was there. The portal before them was not a conventional doorway, but a rectangular opening, its edges ragged, indistinct, and shimmering with an eerie light. It was as though a portion of the wall had melted away leaving a passage.

Sobola stepped through the opening and turned to Bret and his friends still standing cautiously on the other side.

"Well," he growled, "come on in."

Bret and his companions stepped through the opening to find themselves in a brightly-lit rotunda. When the last of Sergeant Carney's troops had stepped through the opening Sobola again touched the stone on his medallion. The soft whirring nose began again and the opening closed in upon itself and disappeared. The wall was now solid; showing no trace of the opening that only seconds before had been there.

* * * * *

The circular wall of the rotunda was of a smooth, gray material similar to the tunnel that led to it. There were no openings in the wall at floor level, but Bret could see several square ports high up encircling the room at the base of the dome. A green light emanated from a circular opening at the top of the dome, casting a glaucous hue over the entire area.

Sobola led Bret and his friends to the center of the room. "I go now to arrange an audience with Lord Vidor," he said. "You'll remain here till he's ready to see you."

Sobola walked away; accompanied by his two guards. He had gone only a few steps when he turned to look at Bret and the others.

"Don't get any foolish ideas," he warned. "If you will look up at the ports along the wall you'll see you're not alone."

Bret and his companions looked to see several men dressed similar to the two with Sobola standing in the openings, their pistols drawn. With a satisfied smirk, Sobola again turned and walked toward the wall. As he approached he touched his medallion and an opening appeared before him. Sobola and his two cohorts stepped through and the opening disappeared.

"Don't try anything foolish he says," Nelda snorted, mocking Sobola. "As if we were going anywhere." She looked up at the guards along the girdle of the dome. "Guess that freak doesn't know ordinary people can't walk through walls like he can," she said.

"I'm sure his power to do that is in the green stone he carries around his neck," Yolette said. "That and the proper amount of concentration."

Bret slipped his arm around her waist. "I'm sure you're right," he said. Yolette smiled contentedly and snuggled closer to Bret. Turning his attention to Sergeant Carney, he continued, "We have to get our hands on one of those things."

"Damn right," he replied. "The first chance we get." Sergeant Carney turned to his men. "Might as well make yourselves comfortable," he told them. "No telling how long that bloke will be gone. Sit if you like." His thirteen troops wearily sank to the floor. Then he, Bret, and the women also sat.

Bret looked toward the base of the dome and studied the uniforms of their captors but could not identify them. They were unlike any culture he had ever heard of. He was confused. Until this point he had assumed the ruler of this evil place was immortal, having lived many centuries, gathering people along the way to populate this dark world of his creation. But if that were the case Bret should have been able to place the strangely dressed men into some approximate era of history. But he couldn't.

Suddenly, a mind-boggling question sprang to mind. If the ruler of this miserable place gathered people from the past to populate the cruel world of his making, could he also visit the future for the same purpose?

Bret looked up at the light emanating from the fixture in the ceiling. Since arriving in this world he had seen only torches and oil lamps. Could it be he asked himself, these people were from a civilization yet to appear in his time? Why not? came the answer without hesitation. After all, from his friends' point of view he would be considered from the future. And, to him, they were from the past. But here there was no past or future, only a constant now. Time, as any of the inhabitants had formerly known it, had no significance here.

Bret shook his head. It's an anomaly with no answer, he told himself and he was determined not to dwell on it.

CHAPTER 11

For Bret and his companions, in the cold stillness of the rotunda, under the watchful eyes of Sobola's guards, time passed slowly. An hour drug by, then another, reinforcing their painful awareness that, for the moment at least, Lord Vidor held their fate in his hands.

Sergeant Carney rose from his sitting position and began to pace. "Where is that bloody little weasel, Sobola?" he snarled and casts a contemptuous glance at the guard ports at the base of the rotunda dome. "What's taking him so long?"

Bret sat with his arms thrust behind his torso supporting his back and his legs trailing out before him. Nonchalantly he rolled his head in a circular motion, his neck emitting an occasional cracking noise.

"Sobola will get back to us when he and Lord Vidor are good and ready," he said casting a glance at the guards above. "Meanwhile those guys up there are supposed to intimidate us." Bret pursed his lips in thought and shrugged his shoulders. "No use getting uptight about it," he said. "It's all part of the psychological warfare."

Carney stopped pacing and walked to where Bret sat and knelt beside him. "What is this psychological warfare?" he asked.

"Oh, you know, he's letting us know who's calling the shots. Lord Vidor wants us to have time to realize how he's got us by the short hairs on a downhill pull."

Carney grinned. "Well," he said, "it's sure not the first time I've been in that situation, I can tell you."

The sergeant's grin disappeared as a soft whirring noise drifted through the rotunda. The sound, by now, was familiar to the captives. It was the sound that preceded the appearance of a portal in solid rock. Sergeant Carney's men rose to their feet and faced the wall awaiting the appearance of the opening.

As the noise grew in intensity a small point of blue light appeared on the stone wall. For a few seconds it danced there, slowly spreading as the tempo of the whirring sound increased. Then the eerie blue light faded in upon itself becoming a ragged hole that quickly expanded into a passage. Sobola and his two men stepped through.

"Lord Vidor has granted you an audience," he said with exaggerated benevolence. "But he suggests you should first be offered refreshment. So, if you will follow me."

Sobola turned and stepped back through the opening in the wall. His two guards stepped toward Bret and his friends and they followed Sobola through the gateway.

* * * * *

On the other side they found themselves in a long hallway lined with brownstone masonry and lit by fixtures in the arched ceiling. As Sobola faced the wall, his amulet in his hand, the portal shrunk and disappeared.

* * * * *

As they traveled the corridor the party passed several conventional doors of heavy timber and iron strapping. Lord Vidor's domain was, apparently equipped with the mysterious passages that appeared and vanished in solid walls only in selected outer areas.

* * * * *

Sobola halted the procession when he reached a set of huge double doors. Like the others in the area, they were of rough timbers reinforced with wide metal straps held in place by crude rivets. A deep booming noise reverberated through the grotto as Sobola pounded on the door with his fist. Slowly they swung inward revealing a cavernous hall strewn with banquet tables and benches.

"Hurry now," Sobola said as he swept through the doorway, "we don't want to keep Lord Vidor waiting any longer than necessary."

* * * * *

Bret and his friends were barely inside the cavern when the double doors behind them were slammed shut with a resounding thud. They whirled to see two small pale figures hefting a wooden bar in place across the doors. They were smaller in stature than Sobola and his men, appearing somewhat frail by comparison. They were extremely light complexioned with soft features, giving them an almost pixy-like countenance.

The two at the door stood with their backs to the portal looking out over the dining hall. They could have easily been mistaken for children except that one was obviously a grown woman of whatever species she represented. Her round, firm breasts, narrow waist, and broad hips left no doubt she was a fully developed, although very small, female. It seemed curious to Bret that she would be performing such heavy duty as gatekeeper. Apparently, he thought, whoever assigned the tasks did so with no regard for gender.

Sobola motioned toward the rows of banquet tables. "Take a seat," he said. "I'm sure you must be hungry."

Sergeant Carney turned to Bret. "What do you think?" he asked.

Bret surveyed the room and the dozen or so elf-like people looking at them. Their large eyes filled with curiosity, they smiled and almost in unison swept their hands toward the tables, also inviting Bret and his companions to sit.

"May as well eat," Bret said. "I don't think they'll try and poison us. If they wanted us dead they could have killed us long ago. Besides, I'm so hungry I could eat a bowl of cold oatmeal smothered in lard."

Carney nodded. "Well," he said with a wry smile, "I could top that. It has to do with the north end of a southbound skunk. And a dead one to boot." He looked at the women and back to Bret. "But in deference to the ladies," he said, "I won't go into it." Then he turned to his men and motioned for them to sit.

Bret sat with Anora at his right and Yolette to his left. Sergeant Carney and Nelda sat across from them while the thirteen remaining members of his command occupied the rest of the table and part of another.

* * * * *

The meal consisted of leafy greens garnished with small chunks of extremely chewy meat. The cross sectional shape of these morsels led Bret to suspect they were bits of snake. But, in his hunger, he didn't dwell on that probability, and, surprisingly, enjoyed the meal.

As one of the female servers offered Sergeant Carney more food her large, soulful eyes made contact with his. Then, casting a furtive glance at the two guards standing against the wall, she leaned closer.

"You and your friends must leave here at once," she whispered softly in his ear. "This place holds only danger for you." She cast another cautious glance at the guards and scurried off.

* * * * *

When dinner was finished Sobola turned to one of the guards accompanying him. He spoke a few words that Bret could not hear and the man walked toward the door. As silently as possible he slipped out. Then Sobola rose to face Bret and the others at the table.

"Only the one who carries his authority on his sleeve and the warlock will come with me to see Lord Vidor," he said. "The others will remain here."

Bret looked down at his flowing robe. In the excitement of recent events he had almost forgotten he was wearing it. I guess he means Sergeant Carney and me, Bret thought.

Nelda rose to hear feet. "Now just a bloomin' minute," she objected. "I'm a member of this party just like anyone else." She drew her sword and glared at Sobola. "And," she went on, "if any a blackhearted jackanapes among your crew doubts I can take care of myself let him step forward."

Sergeant Carney put his hand on Nelda's shoulder and patted it gently.

"Easy, lass," he said. "Let's not commit all our troops at once. We need to keep something in reserve." Nelda looked at Carney, a puzzled expression on her face. "When we go to see this Lord Vidor," he went on, "I want someone guarding my backside I can trust." He gripped her shoulder firmly. "And," he concluded, "that's you."

Nelda grinned. "You can count on me," she said. "I won't let anything happen to your cute little lily-white arse." Carney blushed a deep red but Nelda pretended not to notice as she sheathed her sword and sat.

Sergeant Carney walked to one of his men. "Until I get back," he said, "you're in charge." The rest of his men were close enough to hear the delegation of authority and the man nodded his understanding.

Suddenly the doors opened and several guards poured in led by the man Sobola had sent after them. Silently they took up positions along the wall. Sobola turned to Bret and Carney.

"Now," he said, "you two will come with me."

* * * * *

With his two bodyguards at their backs Bret and Carney followed Sobola from the room and down the hall. Their route took them through several conventional doors, and Sobola did not use the medallion around his neck to open up a passage in the wall.

* * * * *

At length they reached an alcove with a broad, high passage in the far wall. A hooded light hung over the opening revealing a tunnel with a set of railroad tracks running through it. Next to the opening a Trog stood at a console. Lazily he looked up and pulled a lever toward him. Instantly a strange car rolled into view. It was a flatbed with three bench seats, completely covered in transparent material. As the car came to rest the Trog opened a door and stood respectfully to the side.

Sobola motioned Bret and Carney into the strange conveyance, then he and his two men entered. He sat beside Bret and Carney while his two cohorts sat behind them. On his signal the Trog pulled another lever and the car began to roll. At first it moves slowly, but quickly accelerated till the tunnel was flashing by at great speed.

Bret turned to Carney who sat in awed silence, griping the seat tightly, as he fought valiantly, but unsuccessfully, to hold back the expression of panic now spreading across his face. Bret smiled. To a man of the 19th century, he thought, where a vehicle's top speed rarely exceeded 30 miles per hour, this ride, with a velocity easily tripling that, must have been frightening.

In this strange land Bret had come to expect almost anything, and was not too surprised to find that their captors had built a subway within the mountains. The engineering was fairly simple. It utilized existing tunnels connected by short spans excavated from the rock wherever necessary.

The cars were of a dull gray metal framing and large transparent panels. Their unique design gave the rider the feeling of complete detachment from the conveyance as they flashed down the tracks.

Bret's curiosity was piqued by the advanced technology of this world as compared to the one outside. While there the inhabitants lived in a constant dark ages, relying on oil lamps and torches to dispel the darkness of the night, here illumination was provided by incandescent bulbs powered by electricity.

* * * * *

The car decelerated rapidly and pulled to a stop at a raised platform looking out into a spacious cavern. At the edge of the dais a Trog tended a console, barely looking up as the car came to a stop and the occupants got out.

Bret and Sergeant Carney followed Sobola and his guards down the steps and across the grotto. The floor was covered with large vats leaving barely enough room to walk between them. A bank of pink lights was suspended above these vats.

Bret turned to Sergeant Carney. "Well," he said, "now I know where those greens we had for diner came from."

Carney glanced at the tanks and nodded. "These fellows are pretty smart," he said. "They can grow plants underground."

"It's called hydroponic farming," Bret said.

"What?" the sergeant asked, looking intently at the vegetation floating atop the water in the tanks.

"A method of growing things without soil," Bret said. "It was developed in the 20th century sometime in the late 40s or early 50s I believe. But it never really caught on."

Carney looked at the tanks again. "I should think not," he said. "Not as long as there is any land left to farm."

As they walked among the hydroponic tanks Bret and Carney saw they were being tended by people similar to the ones who had waited on them at the meal.

"Who are these little people?" Bret asked Sobola.

Without looking at them, he replied, "We call them Ergs. They tend our gardens and serve us as all manner of domestics."

"And those big hairy blokes?" Carney asked. "What do you call them?"

Sobola shrugged his shoulders. "They are stupid, mindless brutes," he said, "but they are useful at some mundane tasks. Their ability to see in the dark makes them ideal guards for the shadowy outpost regions of the empire. But they have no specific designation."

* * * * *

When Bret and the others reached the opposite side of the cavern he noticed a huge, beetle-like structure clinging to the wall, its six legs disappearing into the stone. It was made of the same dark metal as the subway car, and issued a soft hum.

"What kind of generator is that?" Bret asked, venturing a guess as to the purpose of the object.

Sobola turned to him, a sour look on his face. "A standard piece of equipment," he said. "It draws energy directly from the ground just as any power gatherer."

"But I see no wires attached," Bret said. "How do you get the energy to where you use it?"

"All the equipment we use is attuned to the same frequency as its power gatherer."

"Then, I assume," Bret said, "there is more than one of them."

Sobola smiled and rolled his eyes in a gesture of bored tolerance. "We have many of these machines," he said.

* * * * *

At the other side of the grotto Sobola walked to a small wooden door, almost invisible in the dim light. He produced a key from his belt and inserted it into the lock. The portal creaked open and Bret and Sergeant Carney followed Sobola through the small doorway and headed down a short, well-lighted hall. At the end of the corridor stood a huge door clad in burnished copper, set in a casing of white marble, and flanked by two guards. As Sobola advanced the guards threw open the door and stood aside.

* * * * *

The interior of the apartment glowed with a soft blue light and the floor was covered with a plush carpet. Against the far wall, atop a dais, under a regal canopy a man sat on a throne attended by four guards. Two stood at his right, two at his left.

As Bret and Sergeant Carney were shoved across the floor toward the throne the man rose and glared at them. He was well over six feet, much larger than Sobola and the others they had seen. He began to pace from side to side before the throne, his wiry frame moving with the stealth of a cat, his deep set, expressionless eyes riveted upon them. Then, directly in front of Bret and Carney, he stopped and nonchalantly turned to them.

"I am Lord Vidor," the man said with an air of boredom. "Why have you invaded my kingdom?"

"We didn't mean to invade," Bret said. "We were only looking for a route to the outside."

"Yes," Sergeant Carney joined in. "We had a place a good piece from here. But a cave-in forced us to find an alternate route to the outside. If you'd be so kind as to show us the way out of these mountains we'd be much obliged and be on our way."

Lord Vidor returned to his throne and sat. He leaned back and drummed his fingers on the arms of the throne. Then he leaned forward and spoke to Sobolo.

"You say there were others?" he asked.

"Yes, my lord," Sobola replied sweeping his arm in the direction of Sergeant Carney. "Thirteen dressed as he is and three females."

Lord Vidor smiled. "Females, you say?" Sobola nodded.

Bret stepped forward. "Lord Vidor," he began, "I know you're a busy man and I don't mean to interrupt. But if you could direct us out of these tunnels we'll be on our way. We won't bother you any longer."

Lord Vidor turned to Bret. "You will never leave this place," he said. Then turning back to Sobola he continued. "Take them away. Put them and the others in the holding area till I decide what do with them."

CHAPTER 12

On Sobola's signal his guards drew their weapons and leveled them at Bret and Sergeant Carney.

"Take these two to the holding place," he told his men. "I go to get the others."

Bret and Carney stepped forward as the guards prodded them in the back with the muzzles of their pistols. Quickly they were ushered from the apartment into the hallway. The guards at the door slammed the huge portal shut and stood before it in a defiant stance.

"Take them away," Sobola told his guards. "And tell the keeper of the holding place Lord Vidor has plans for these two. So, although they will have their usual freedom to abuse them, they must stop short of killing them. Lord Vidor has reserved that pleasure for himself."

Sobola smiled as he watched Bret and Sergeant Carney being marched away. Then he turned and hurried back up the corridor toward the dining hall where the three women and Sergeant Carney's men waited.

* * * * *

Anora, Yolette, Nelda, and the men of the lost battalion turned eagerly toward the door as it creaked open. But when only Sobola entered any hope of being on their way out of the mountain was dashed. Since he had left with Bret and Sergeant Carney and was now alone, treachery on his part was obvious. But armed only with bayonets fixed on empty rifles Carney's men knew they were no match for the guards surrounding them.

Nelda glared at Sobola and gripped the handle of her sword. For a moment the instincts acquired through years of piracy seized her mind and urged her to attack. But her better judgement prevailed and she realized that with the armed guards surrounding them it would be suicide. Begrudgingly she accepted the reality of the situation.

Sobola stood for a moment surveying the prisoners. Slowly his gaze passed from one to the other, his lips parting in a lecherous leer as his eyes fell upon the women. The three returned his gaze with withering, icy, contemptuous looks.

"You will all drop your weapons and come with me," he ordered.

Carney's troops unslung their rifles but did not drop them. Instead they held them at the ready, the tips of their bayonets pointed at Sobola's guards as they advanced.

The man Sergeant Carney had left in charge, his rifle still slung, turned to his companions, his hand raised in a signal for restraint.

"Easy lads," he said. "No chance of getting close enough to those blokes do use our bayonets before they cut us down with their side arms. For the moment we have no choice but to surrender to a superior force." He unslung his rifle from his shoulder and dropped it to the floor with a clatter. Their faces reflecting bitter disappointment, the others followed suit. "But we'll have our day," he assured them. "We can hardly escape from here if we're dead now can we?"

* * * * *

The burnished double copper doors leading to the main gallery where Lord Vidor held court glowed softly in the reflected light of the wide hallway. As Sobola approached the massive portal the guards beside it swung open the doors and he entered. Inside, he quickly descended the five marble steps to the main floor and strode toward the throne atop the platform at the other end of the room.

It was a larger version of the throne in Lord Vidor's quarters, and much more ornate. Several retainers hovered nearby as he listened to their flattery and received reports from his personal guard concerning the arrest of the intruders.

Lord Vidor looked up when he heard the door close behind Sobola. He waved the others away as his chief advisor neared the throne. Sobola moved close to Lord Vidor and spoke in low tones.

"Have you decided how you will dispose of the intruders?" he asked.

Vidor rubbed his chin in thought. "What would you suggest?" he asked, answering Sobola's question with a question as he often did.

"It should be something more spectacular than a simple execution," Sobola suggested. "Something that will leave a lasting impression on your subjects. Why not declare a holiday to commemorate the deaths of the strangers? Gather the Ergs, the hairy beasts, and your personal guard together to witness their deaths by some ingeniously evil method."

Lord Vidor shrugged his shoulders. "What possible difference can it make how the prisoners are done away with?" he asked. "Dead is dead. And they'll be no further threat to me."

"True," Sobola agreed, "but their deaths could be used to avert another possible threat."

"What threat?"

"None apparent at this time, but a potential one among the Ergs and the hairy beasts."

"But they're well under control, aren't they?"

"At present. But the appearance of the strangers has, no doubt, roused the curiosity of the Ergs and set them wondering what lies beyond your realm."

"You may be right," Lord Vidor agreed.

"There is always the possibility they may become discontent. Maybe even to the point of rebellion. But if the death of the strangers were handled properly it would discourage any such action."

Lord Vidor pursed his lips in thought. Then a broad grin spread across his face.

"You're right," he said. "These strangers must serve as an example to the Ergs and hairy beasts, as well as my personal guards. And it must be done in the most public way."

"Trust me, their fate will be severe enough to dissuade any of your subjects from attempting to leave."

"Good," Lord Vidor said. "The disposition of these interlopers must leave a lasting impression on the Ergs and the hairy beasts, as well as my own guard."

"I believe your personal guard is above reproach, for the time being," Sobola said. "They still think it was your doing that brought them here after the failed coup."

Lord Vidor smiled broadly. "Yes," he said with a snicker, "they believed me when I told them so. But they were not the intelligentsia elite in the world we left behind nor are they in this one either."

"True," Sobola agreed. "They bungled the mission of eliminating the council and led the authorities straight to us." Sobola paused to smile. "Too bad," he mused, "it would have been the most significant happening of the 26th century.

"They still think that blinding white plasma flash in the eradication chamber was something I did to bring them here to avoid prison," Vidor said. "So their loyalty is pretty well assured."

"But, still," Sobola said, "the appearance of these strangers may set them to wonder what's outside these caverns."

"We can't have that," Lord Vidor said. "If they should wander into the outside world it would displease our benefactor."

"True," Sobola agreed. "Your covenant with the wizard who lives in the castle in the lake of fire clearly states that you are to confine your activities to these caverns. He has given you free rein to torment the Ergs and the hairy ones as you wish. But if they should begin wandering out . . . "

Lord Vidor shuddered and pulled his regal ermine cape closer about his neck.

"I don't even want to think about that," he said.

"If you will but leave everything to me, my lordship I shall see that such a tragedy never comes to pass."

Vidor grinned. "I leave the details to you," he said. "I'm sure you'll come up with something amusing."

Sobola rubbed his hands together in anticipation. "I'll not disappoint you," he promised. "I think," he mused, "we shall begin with the women."

* * * * *

Bret and Sergeant Carney tugged at the huge metal rings in the center of the solid wooden door. But it was an exercise in futility, serving only to vent anger and frustration.

When Bret and the others were herded into the dank cell, the heavy portal slammed shut, and the bolt thrown there was little hope of escape. Through the small barred port at the top of the door they could see the anteroom outside where two of Sobola's guards sat at a table beside the door leading to the hallway outside. The rifles taken from Carney and his men, bayonets still fixed, were stacked in the corner.

Bret heaved a sigh, sank to the floor, and leaned back against the door. "It won't budge," he said.

"Nary an inch," Carney agreed. He stood slightly stooped with his hands on his knees, breathing deeply. "It looks like Sparkle was right," he said.

"Who's Sparkle," Anora asked.

Carney smiled. "Oh," he said, "that's what I call one of those little creatures that served us lunch."

Yolette smiled. "They do sort of sparkle with their large eyes and milky complexion," she said.

"What did you mean, Sparkle was right?" Nelda asked.

Sergeant Carney grinned. "When she offered me more food she warned that we were in danger and should get away from here," he said.

"Excellent advice," Bret said. "I suggest we follow it at our first opportunity."

"If we ever get out of here," Yolette said.

"We will," Bret replied with authority.

"Of course we will," Carney concurred. He looked at his men sitting on the floor against the far wall of the cell. "All of us," he added.

"Does anyone have a plan?" Nelda asked.

"The guards will have to open the door sometime," Bret reasoned. "Unless they intend to starve us they'll have to bring us food. There's no room to pass it under the door and the port at the top is barred."

"Right you are," Sergeant Carney agreed. "But I'm sure only one of the guards will come to the door at any given time. When we get our chance we'll have to move fast. If one of those blokes gets close enough to me so I can get hold of his sidearm the other one will be an easy target."

* * * * *

Bret and Carney moved to the cell door as they heard the one to the antechamber open on squeaky hinges. Looking through the small barred port they saw one of the pixy-like creatures standing at the guard desk outside. Siting at her feet was a covered bucket with a long handled ladle hanging from the bail.

The guards watching her every movement with cold indifference, she sat a bowl in front of each and placed a spoon alongside it. Then she lifted the bucket and sat it on the corner of the table and filled the bowls.

"It's Sparkle," Sergeant Carney said.

"How can you tell?" Bret asked. "They all look pretty much alike to me."

"But I'm sure that's the one who warned me we were in trouble."

"You know, sergeant, you have a real knack for gathering useful information," Nelda said sarcastically, patting Carney on the back in a mock congratulatory gesture. "It seems your little friend was right." Nelda patted the sergeant on the shoulder. "Maybe she can tell us how to get out of here," she concluded.

Carney ignored her jibes and watched the guards wolf down their food. When they were finished one wiped his slobbery lips on his sleeve, belched loudly, rose from the table, and walked toward the cell. He peered through the opening at the top of the portal. With a crooked sneer he stepped back and kicked the door violently.

"Get away from the door," he ordered. "Stand back into the cell where I can see you all. Your food is here but I'll not open the door till you stand back."

When the prisoners moved away from the door the key turned in the lock and the door swung open, the rusty hinges issuing a raspy, high-pitched squeak. Sparkle entered carrying the bucket and the door slammed shut behind her.

"Make it fast," the guard snarled.

Sparkle set the bucket down and smiled. "Your food," she said and dipped the ladle into the bucket and withdrew it filled with a green gruel. "I'm afraid you'll have to share the ladle," she apologized. "Sobola will not allow a separate one for each of you. He says it's too much of a temptation for prisoners to conceal one and make it into a weapon. Also, it is not necessary for the guards to remember how many I entered the cell with. They have only to see that I have one when I leave." Sparkle grinned. "Anything more complicated would tax the mentality of the guards," she said.

Bret grinned and nodded. "Well," he said, turning to the woman, "we might as well dine. Ladies first."

As the prisoners ate the gruel, a liquidized version of the greens they had had earlier, Sparkle spoke in hushed tones.

"Lore Vidor is planning to make a spectacle of your deaths," she said.

"How do you know that?" Bret asked. "How do you know he is planning to kill us at all?"

"I have a friend who works as a chambermaid for the lord in his living quarters as well as in the main gallery."

"Main gallery?" Anora repeated.

"Yes. The large room where Lord Vidor holds court. The main throne room."

"He has more than one?" Sergeant Carney asked, a smile on his lips. "How many thrones can one bloke sit on anyway?"

"He has two," Sparkle replied. "A very large, fancy one in the main gallery where he holds court and a smaller one in his sleeping quarters. It's my friend's duty to keep both places neat. And in the course of her duties she has overheard things."

"What sort of things?" Bret asked.

"As I said, Lord Vidor plans to make an example of you and your friends. He views your presence here as a threat to his tyrannical rule and has declared a holiday in observance of your execution."

"Sound to me," Nelda said, "like Lord Vidor isn't too well loved around here."

"He is feared by the Ergs and hairy ones. He remains in power by force of his guards who are known for their ruthlessness and sadistic nature."

"Can you get us out of here?" Bret asked.

Sparkle looked into space, sadness in her eyes. "I could disable the guards and get you out of this cell," she said. "But I could do nothing more to help."

"Fair enough. Just get us out of this cell and we'll do the rest."

"I can do nothing till tomorrow afternoon."

"Why not?" Yolette asked.

"I'll be working in the kitchen tomorrow until mid-afternoon," Sparkle replied. "Someone else will be bringing the morning and midday meal to the guards. I'll be back around this time late tomorrow to deliver their evening meal. The food will be laced with a certain plant that grows wild in the darker recesses of the caverns. When the guards eat them they should be unconscious within minutes. Death will occur in a matter of hours." Sparkle looked at Sergeant Carney, a pleading look in her huge eyes. "Lord Vidor will know it was I that helped you escape," she said. "Please take me with you when you leave here."

Carney looked at Bret who nodded his agreement. The sergeant put his hand gently on Sparkle's shoulder.

"Sure we'll take you with us," he said.

* * * * *

It was well into the next day when Sobola, along with a dozen guards, entered the anteroom of the dungeon.

"Open the cell," he ordered. "Lord Vidor wants the women brought to him. They must be properly prepared for the upcoming ceremony."

When the guard unlocked the door and swung it wide Bret and Sergeant Carney stood in front of the women.

"They aren't going anywhere without us," Carney declared. "If you want them you'll have to go through us to get them."

Sobola glanced over his shoulder at the guards backing him up. "Don't be fools," he sneered. "The women are going with me whether you are alive or dead."

Anora slipped her arm around Bret's waist and hugged his tightly. "There's nothing you can do against such odds," she whispered in his ear. "Especially when they're armed and you aren't. Better to wait till Sparkle sets you all free. Then, with the element of surprise on your side, we'll all get out of here."

Bret looked at Sergeant Carney. He had been standing close enough to hear Anora's whispers and nodded his agreement. Begrudgingly the two men stepped aside. Two of Sobola's guards moved forward and led Anora, Nelda, and Yolette from the cell.

CHAPTER 13

The women were escorted to an apartment next to the main gallery. Although the room was small it was tastefully decorated in a feminine motif. The walls were hung with colorful tapestries and a large carpet covered most of the marble floor. There was a bowl of fruit on a table just inside the door and across the room a large canopied bed sat against the wall.

"I'm afraid you'll find the accommodations somewhat inadequate," Sobola apologized sarcastically. "The apartment will be a little cramped for three. But you won't be here that long. And the place is normally occupied by only one woman at a time."

"I see," Nelda said as she scanned the room. "And I'll bet she's not here just to turn down the bloody sheets either. His nibs' little love nest, heigh what?"

"His lordship prefers the term harem," Sobola said. "Although it is somewhat of a misnomer since, as I said, only one woman occupies the premises at any given time."

"Nevertheless," Nelda said, "I'm sure we can make do with the small quarters."

"But your inconvenience will be short-lived, I assure you," Sobola continued. He motioned toward an archway across the room. "The bath is through there," he said. "You may use it or not, it's up to you. It's of no consequence to me or Lord Vidor." Sobola pointed to the bed. "For your appearance before him tomorrow you will wear the clothing you find there," he ordered.

Sullenly, the women walked to the bed. Anora picked up a garment from one of the piles there. Her lips set in a sour expression; she held it before her and glared at Sobola.

"This is a harem outfit," she said. "This loony boss of yours really believes in carrying things to the extreme, doesn't he?" She dropped the garment to the bed as though it was something of absolutely no value to her. "If he thinks I'm going to wear that," she said in a measured tone laden with revulsion, "he's crazy."

Nelda picked up another costume and held it at arm's length. "We'd look like a bunch of bloody belly dancers in these," she said with disgust.

"You are not required to like them," Sobola said. "You are only required to wear them."

"And if we choose not to?" Nelda asked defiantly.

"Then you will be dressed in them by force," Sobola blurted. He looked at his guards, then back to the women and grinned. "I don't think I'd have any trouble finding volunteers among my men for the job," he said.

"What does Lord Vidor plan to do with us?" Yolette asked. "And why these ridiculous costumes?"

"The reason for the costumes is obvious," Anora said. "This imbecilic despot must think he's Aladdin or Sinbad or some such character from The Arabian Nights."

"Tomorrow you three will provide entertainment at the gathering in the main gallery," Sobola said, ignoring the woman's outburst.

"Entertainment?" Anora repeated questioningly. "What kind of entertainment?"

"Lord Vidor is an avid aficionado of the ancient mid-eastern art of belly dancing."

"Are you serious?" Nelda asked. "Does that crazy bloke really expect us to dance for him in these skimpy things?"

"He does," Sobola snapped in a stern voice. Then, softening his tone, he continued. "And when I tell you of a special stage I'm having built just for your performance I'm sure you'll be happy to oblige."

Anora looked at Sobola, a suspicious glint in her eyes. "What do you mean?" she asked.

Sobola heaved a contented sigh and gazed into space, obviously quite pleased with his self.

"I'm having constructed an elevated, circular stage in front of the throne," he said, tracing a large circle in the air with his hands. "It'll be completed by early afternoon tomorrow.

"In keeping with the theme of your dress, Arabian music will be provided by selections from Lord Vidor's extensive personal library. You will dance for him to this music." Sobola grinned. "Oh," he continued, "did I mention the stage will be made of metal?" He grinned again. "If your dancing is pleasing to Lord Vidor," he said, "all will be well for you. But each time you displease him you will receive an electric shock through your bare feet." Sobola paused to momentarily relish the image he had created. Then his eyes narrowed as he glared at the women. "Each succeeding shock will be more intense," he growled. "If you displease Lord Vidor five times, on the sixth occasion the stage will tilt on a central pivot and you will fall into a vat of acid underneath." Sobola rubbed his hands together in perverse glee. "The vat, of course, will be glass," he said almost in a giggle. "All assembled in the great gallery will be able to see your futile attempts to escape as your bodies slowly disintegrate." Sobola paused to look at the women's faces. "So," he said, "I would suggest you do all in your power to please the lord. You will not only be prolonging your own existence but that of your companions as well."

"What do you mean by that?" Yolette asked.

"Oh, did I neglect to tell you of their fate?" Sobola asked with mock concern. "After your, shall we say, performance, they will be put, one at a time, on the stage. When the lock is released it will be interesting to see how long they can maintain its critical balance before it tips, dropping them into the vat of acid."

Anora frowned. "All right," she said. "You win. We'll play the maniac's crazy game."

Sobola nodded. "Until tomorrow," he said. "I will come for you when we are ready for you in the main gallery." He looked at the costumes lying on the bed. "You had better be properly dressed," he warned. Then with a sneer he turned and strode from the apartment followed closely by his guards. The heavy wooden door slammed shut with an ominous thud.

Nelda picked up the harem costume again and held it in front of her. "Well," she said, "things could be worse, I suppose."

"Not much," Anora said. "We'll have to appear in those skimpy things before Lord Vidor and who knows who else." Anora shook her head. "It'll be so degrading," she concluded.

Nelda dropped the costume to the bed. "Lord Vidor intends to kill us," she said. "I'm sure of that. But he wants to toy with us a bit first. The longer we prolong things the better. Bret and Sergeant Carney and his men are our only hope of rescue, but they can't possibly get here till late tomorrow afternoon. So we have to keep things really interesting for those blokes till then."

"You're right," Anora said. "It's our only hope."

"But I have no idea how to do what that vile man wants me to do," Yolette said.

"I've seen belly dancers in Madagascar and French Morocco," Nelda said. "We have till tomorrow to teach you both how to do it." She picked up the costume again and looked at it, noting its flimsiness. Then with a smile she swiveled her hips several times and thrust her pelvis forward. "Just wait till those blokes get an eyeful of me in this," she said. "Those belly dancers I've seen in North Africa won't have a thing on me."

* * * * *

It was late in the afternoon of the following day when Sparkle appeared in the anteroom of the dungeon with her bucket of gruel. She sat bowls before the guards and ladled the green matter into them. Quickly they devoured it.

"What's the special event in the main gallery today?" Sparkle asked. She knew full well what was being planned but was playing for time to allow the poison in the food to work. Usually, after she fed the guards she would be locked in the cell while she fed the prisoners. But she could not allow that today. If the poison took effect with her in the cell she would be as much a prisoner as those she was trying to free. With the changing of the guard, when they found their dead comrades, her culpability would be obvious. Then not only would there be no escape, but she would be executed for her part in the attempt.

The guards looked at Sparkle with sullen contempt. "Time to feed them," one snorted, cocking his head in the direction of the cell door.

"They can wait," Sparkle said. "I'd rather talk to you two. I'm curious about the special event. And if anyone would know about it it would be two well informed gentlemen like you." The guards looked at Sparkle with a blank stare that told her the poison was beginning to have an effect on them. "Do you know what the special event is to be?" she asked.

"You'll know when you see it," one of the guards said. "You Ergs will be required to watch it, whatever it is."

"Yes," Sparkle said, "I'm aware of that. I just thought you might be able to give me an idea of what to expect."

"We don't know ourselves, except that the strangers are to be done away with. But it will not be a simple execution. Lord Vidor has promised something highly entertaining."

"Enough talk," the other guards said. "Feed the prisoners and be gone."

As he started to rise he fell back into his chair. For a moment he looked at Sparkle with glazed eyes, then pitched forward onto the table. Silently, his companion turned toward him, a bewildered look on his face. Then he, too, fell forward onto the table.

Quickly Sparkle picked up the keys from the table and opened the cell door.

"We must hurry," she said as Bret and the others poured out. "The ceremony will start within the hour in the main gallery."

"Lead on," Bret said.

Sparkle slowly opened the door leading from the dungeon anteroom and stepped out into the dimly lit corridor. She peered intently in both directions; her eyes long accustomed to darkness piercing the shadows, then turned back toward the door.

"The area is deserted," she said.

Bret and Sergeant Carney stepped into the corridor. Cautiously they looked in both directions.

"Let's get on with it," Carney said. "The sooner we engage the enemy the better."

Nodding silently Sparkle led the way, Bret and Carney at her side, and the sergeant's troops following close behind.

* * * * *

After several anxious minutes and numerous turns in the shadowy corridor Sparkle led them to a small alcove. She put her small hands on the wall and pushed. There was a scraping sound and a section of the wall began to move inward.

"This leads to the main gallery, as well as other places," Sparkle said.

"Are you sure you can lead us to the main gallery?" Bret asked.

"Yes," Sparkle confirmed. "And we will enter directly behind the throne. There is no door to the passage there. It's hidden by a tapestry." Her pixy-like face lit up with amusement. "It was designed so," she continued, "in case Lord Vidor should need to make a hasty exit for some reason." Her smile broadened. "I find that ironic, don't you?" she asked.

Bret smiled. "Poetic justice," he mused. "What he designed to protect himself will help us kick his ass before he knows we're anywhere near him."

Sparkle smiled and entered the dark passage. "Come," she said softly. "The way is dark, but I will lead you."

Bret, Sergeant Carney, and his men followed. With a grinding noise the passage swung shut.

* * * * *

The door to the apartment burst open and Sobola, along with four guards, strode in. Anora, Nelda, and Yolette sat on the bed dressed in the harem costumes.

They rose as Sobola entered. For a moment he stood looking at them, a smile of approval on his lips.

"It's time for your performance," he snickered.

Nelda stepped forward to confront the man. "What of our friends?" she asked. "Will they be there?"

"Guards are on their way to fetch them?" Sobola replied. Then, with a crooked sadistic smile, he went on. "Don't fret," he said. "They should be there in plenty of time to see your grand finale."

"By the way," Nelda said with a pleasant smile, "I probably won't get a chance later so I'll say it now. You and that slimy blackguard, Lord Vidor, can both kiss my bloody rosy-red arse."

Sobola lashed out with the back of his hand, catching Nelda on the cheek with a stinging blow. Her head spun to the side but she remained standing. With a contemptuous grin she spat on the floor.

"If Lord Vidor was not expecting three women to dance for him," Sobola threatened, "I'd take great pleasure in killing you." He motioned to the guards to escort the women from the room. "But," he mused, "seeing you squirm on the stage I've had constructed for you and your eventual plunge into the acid vat will be just as satisfying."

CHAPTER 14

The main gallery was filled to capacity. The hairy creatures Bret and his friends called Trogs stood along the walls on both sides of the room. Unaccustomed to the bright light, they repeatedly blinked their outer eyelids while the inner, dark membrane protecting their large, bovine eyes made them appear as blackened, empty sockets. Their ragged lines ranging from four or five to a dozen deep ran from the double doors on one end of the room to where Lord Vidor sat on his throne atop the dais at the other.

Because of their smaller size Sobola had the Ergs placed in the center of the room so the large hairy creatures would not obstruct their view of the proceedings.

On the main floor, their backs to the dais, a line of Lord Vidor's guards stood facing the crowd. Directly in front of them sat a large, circular glass cauldron standing six feet high and over eight feet across. It was filled nearly to overflowing with acid and topped with a tilting metal stage.

Between the vat and the crowd stood three additional ranks of guards stretching from wall to wall. Sobola stood beside the vat looking out over the crowd. The docile Ergs stood silent; almost reverently awaiting whatever Lord Vidor had assembled them to witness. However, the Trogs were beginning to mill about and conversing in their peculiar language of whistles and moans.

They are a stupid lot, Sobola thought. With so many assembled in one place they may cause trouble. Then he grinned as he surveyed his guards. No, he told himself, not even those stupid brutes would go against my guards and certain death.

The murmur of the crowd was hushed as the massive double doors opened and Lord Vidor entered. Surrounded by his personal guard of six men he made his way through the crowd toward the dais. He wore a conceited look of self importance as the crowd parted to let him pass.

With great ceremony he mounted the ornate staircase to the dais, walked smugly to his throne, and sat. With a nonchalant wave of his hand he sent his personal guard to join the others on the floor. While Lord Vidor surveyed the room, Sobola left his post near the vat and mounted the staircase to the dais. Respectfully he approached the throne and leaned down to whisper to Lord Vidor.

"My lord," he said, "you will note the small box attached to the right arm of the throne." Lord Vidor placed his hand on it and nodded. "As we discussed," Sobola continued, "the women will dance for you. When you are displeased with their performance you may punish them. To deliver a shock, push the red button. The current will continue as long as you keep the button depressed."

Lord Vidor grinned. "And of course," he said, "no matter how well they dance they will displease me at times." His grin broadened. "Otherwise," he confided, "how will I experience the pleasure of their pain?"

Sobola nodded. "Exactly my lord," he said. "And when you tire of their performance press the blue button. That will release the locking device that holds the stage horizontal. It will tilt on a central axis, dumping them into the acid."

Lord Vidor put his hand on Sobola's shoulder and drew him close. "You're an evil man," he smirked. "Maybe as evil as I." Lord Vidor regarded Sobola with a suspicious air. "Are you also an ambitious one?" he asked. "Should I be on my guard?"

Sobola smiled. "No need for that my lord," he said. "I'm quite content with my station in life."

Lord Vidor looked Sobola up and down, one eyebrow raised in a superior attitude.

"Good," he said. Then in a sarcastic tone he continued. "In that case there is no need for you to share the dais with me. Bring on the entertainment. Then return to your station on the floor and make sure the guards keep their eyes sharp."

Sobola nodded humbly, stepped from the dais, and walked to the other end of the great hall, signaling the guards to throw open the double entrance doors.

With him in the lead, amid great fanfare, Anora, Nelda, and Yolette were forced across the gallery toward the leering Lord Vidor. As they neared the vat two guards pushed a narrow wooden stairway against it. When the women had ascended onto the stage it was taken away. The choking fumes from the acid rose to sting their nostrils and burn their eyes. Sobola took up a position next to the vat and faced the crowd, his sour look daring anyone to object to the proceedings.

From an unseen source music began to fill the room. On the metal stage atop the acid cauldron the women begrudgingly started to dance. Lord Vidor settled back on his throne, enjoying the spectacle as they moved their hips in time with the throb of drums, the hypnotic wail of flutes, and the clash of cymbals.

The sheer, diaphanous material of their costumes allowed Arnor's and Nelda's breasts to jiggle and their nipples to thrust out prominently. Yolette's small, firm bosom did not move as her friends' did but her hip and pelvic movements in the dance were just as erotic.

* * * * *

Inside the secret passage Bret halted, listening intently. "What's that?" he questioned. "It sounds like music."

"It is," Sparkle said. "I've heard it many times before. We must hurry. Lord Vidor accompanies all his public punishments with that music."

"How much farther?" Sergeant Carney asked.

"Not far," Sparkle replied. "We're almost there."

"How can you tell? It's so bloody dark in here I wouldn't have the foggiest where we are. I can barely see my bloomin' hand in front of me."

"My eyes are more suited to seeing in the dark than yours," Sparkle said. "And since the music doesn't carry far through these thick walls we must be getting close to our goal."

* * * * *

Lord Vidor grinned and pushed the red button. The women cried out and jerked first one foot then the other off the stage. But there was no way they could avoid the punishing jolt of electricity. Lord Vidor laughed uproariously at the women's pain then released the button.

"Come now," he chided, "that was but a small taste of what is to come if you don't please me. Continue your dance."

Anora, Nelda, and Yolette glared hatefully at the grinning Vidor and slowly resumed their swaying in time to the music.

Across the gallery the massive double doors swung open and four guards entered. The leader of the group scanned the hall, searching for Sobola. Seeing him standing beside the acid vat he led the other three through the crowd toward him.

As the guards approached Sobola scowled. "Where are the men prisoners?" he demanded.

"They have escaped," the leader of the four guards said in a low tone.

"What!"

"They must have had help from someone," the guard alibied. "The dungeon watch were both dead."

"Dead? How?"

"I'm not sure. There were no marks on them."

Sobola's eyebrows knitted in anger. "Well I can tell you exactly what happened," he snorted. "That Erg that brings their food poisoned them. There can be no other answer."

Anora, Nelda, and Yolette watched the exchange between Sobola and the guard. They couldn't hear what was being said. But from Sobola's expression and highly animated manner they knew the news brought by the guard did not please him. Amused, they became so engrossed in watching Sobola in his frustration that without realizing it they slowed their gyrations nearly to a standstill.

"Dance, damn you!" Lord Vidor snarled as he leaned forward in his throne and pressed the red button, holding it down for several seconds.

The women screamed and hopped on one foot then the other as the current surged through their bodies. When Vidor released the button they collapsed on the stage.

"Dance, you trollops!" Vidor shouted.

The women rose and resumed their dance with more vigor than before.

"Make it good," Nelda whispered. "Whatever that guard told Sobola can't be good for our cause. We don't want our performance cut short for more pressing matters. Whatever happens we have to keep his nibs interested."

"I have a feeling," Anora replied in a low voice, "Lord Vidor intends to kill us no matter what. It just depends on how long it takes him to tire of this farce."

"You're right about that," Nelda said. "That's why we have to keep him interested till Bret and the others get here."

"Three more shocks and we're goners," Anora said.

"Then we bloody well can't let that happen," Nelda declared. "If it looks like he's getting bored we'll have to do whatever it takes to keep him interested."

"It seems he's only interested in torturing us, and eventually killing us," Yolette said. "And I'm not sure I can withstand three more shocks."

"Then we'll have to make sure things don't go that far."

"How?" Yolette asked.

"If he looks like he's getting bored I'll show him a bare tit. If I know men, and I think I do, he'll be wanting to see the other one, and Anora's as well. That should buy us a little time."

"I wish Bret and Sergeant Carney would hurry," Yolette said.

"They'll be here," Anora assured her.

Lord Vidor pushed the red button again, holding it down, prolonging the shock delivered to the women. They cried out and again fell to the stage their legs jerking uncontrollably with involuntary spasms.

Vidor chuckled and slapped his thigh in glee. Then he rose from his throne and walked to the front of the dais. There, on a level with the women, he glared at them as they painfully rose to their feet.

"No talking," he snarled. "You were talking. I don't like that. I want you to dance, not talk."

* * * * *

Bret, Sparkle, Sergeant Carney, and his men had reached their destination directly behind the dais and now stood at the archway. On Carney's signal his men slipped silently through the opening and spread out along the wall behind the massive tapestry. The sound of their stealthy footsteps was not heard over the throb of the music and the slight ruffle of the tapestry not noticed as all eyes in the great gallery were fixed on the women dancing atop the vat of acid.

Sergeant Carney let out a fierce cry. In unison his men tore down the tapestry and with him in the lead lunged across the dais and leaped to the floor of the gallery. In spread formation they charged the rank of guards like a frenzied mob gone mad. To Sergeant Carney and his men it was total war, no quarter asked and none given. Any target, whether facing or turned away, was fair game. Screaming insults at the top of their lungs they thrust and slashed with their bayonets and lashed out with the butts of their rifles.

Taken by surprise, several guards fell before the onslaught before they could turn to face the attack and their ranks were severely depleted by the assault. Now at close quarters, they could not halt, or even slow the lethal Juggernaut of flashing bayonets and crashing rifle butts.

The three ranks of Sobola's guards in front of the vat whirled to the sound of Sergeant Carney's battle cry. They drew their side arms and started toward the dais to aid their comrades.

Suddenly the hairy creatures began shrieking and forcing their way through the crowd of Ergs toward the guards. Sobola and his men were now caught between the bayonets of Sergeant Carney's men and the outraged creatures they had so badly abused in the past.

At the sound of the commotion behind them the guards turned to see the Ergs giving way to the tide of Trogs rushing toward them. The forward rank had time to fire only one volley from their side arms before the hairy creatures were upon them. Several Trogs fell but the charge was not blunted. Others, their rage now increased, leaped over the prostrate bodies to clash with the guards.

Lord Vidor's men were no match for the hairy beasts with their larger size and superior strength. With low, rumbling snarls the Trogs smashed into the crumbling ranks of Vidor's guard. The great hall rang with their screams as the Trogs locked their mighty arms around them in punishing bearhugs, jerking them off the floor, and snapping their spines. Others died more quietly as the hairy beasts throttled them with their large, powerful hands.

Lord Vidor whirled and ran toward the box on the arm of his throne. Vengefully he pushed the blue button unlocking the stage, hoping to dump the women into the vat of acid. But he was too late. The moment he turned his back to make his way to the throne the women leaped to the floor. In the melee, with Sobola and his men caught between two avenging forces, they hugged the glass cauldron.

In the din of battle as Sobola looked around frantically, searching for a way of escape, he caught sight of the women. Suddenly he realized that escape might be possible with one of them as a hostage. Stealthily he moved to Nelda and pushed the barrel of his sidearm into her ribs.

But before Sobola could put his plan into action Sergeant Carney, wielding his bayonet nearby, saw that Nelda was in danger. With renewed ferocity he fought his way through the few remaining guards toward Sobola.

"Leave her alone!" he shouted.

Sobola turned his weapon on Carney, but was not fast enough. With a powerful thrust the sergeant sank his bayonet into Sobola's stomach.

"You bastard," Carney shouted as he jerked his bayonet out with a ripping sound.

The stunned look on Sobola's face turned slowly to hatred as he sank to his knees. His life threading out, in his weakness, his head pitched forward and his tiara clattered to the floor. It rolled toward Nelda standing with her back to the acid vat.

Near death, Sobola watched as she picked up the coronal symbol of his authority. His lips moved in a silent curse, then he pitched forward, dead.

In the mass confusion Lord Vidor made a lunge for the escape route behind the throne. But he had made it only a few steps when Bret grabbed him from behind. He spun the terrified despot around and dragged him back onto the dais. In the scuffle the chain holding the medallion he wore was broken and it fell to the floor.

In his rage and frustration Vidor didn't notice the loss, but lashed out with a looping right cross. Bret easily ducked under it and countered with a stinging right jab to Vidor's nose. His eyes glazed over as the blood spurted from his nostrils and covered his upper lip. Bret threw a hard right cross that connected with Lord Vidor's jaw. He staggered back across the dais but was able to stay on is feet. Pressing his advantage Bret pursued his groggy adversary and delivered a crashing left uppercut.

The blow caught Lord Vidor directly on the chin. Now at the edge of the dais, he was catapulted onto the metal stage atop the glass cauldron. Momentarily the stage teetered as he scrambled to reach the side. Then, under his weight, the stage tilted and with a scream he slid into the acid.

His arms flailing, his legs thrashing, he plunged to the bottom of the vat. The clear acid turned a muddled gray as it began to eat into his flesh. The surface of the vat began to seethe and give off a blue choking vapor.

Vidor fought his way to the surface, his mouth open but no sound came out. In a feeble effort to escape he beat his fists against the metal stage overhead. Then slowly he sank to the bottom of the cauldron, now barely recognizable; his body beginning to disintegrate as the acid consumed it.

The din of battle now subsiding, Nelda and Yolette ran to Bret's side on the dais. As they looked out over the hall the Trogs, their anger vented, began to move from the center toward the side walls. The dead and dying of the brief but deadly encounter lay strewn on the floor. The Ergs, who had fled to the relative safety of the side walls while the battle raged returned to the center of the gallery.

Sparkle picked up the medallion Lord Vidor had lost during his brief scuffle with Bret. Slowly she walked to the front of the dais and surveyed the carnage. Then she raised the medallion high, thrusting it out toward the crowd. A spontaneous cheer erupted form the Ergs. The Trogs thrust their fists into the air and grunted their approval.

Nelda walked to Sparkle's side and placed Sobola's tiara on her head. The great hall rang with another cheer. Sparkle graciously accepted the tribute with a modest bow.

Smiling broadly, Nelda returned to stand with her friends. Slipping her arm around Bret's waist she beamed at him.

"The king is dead," she said. "Long live the queen."

Bret nodded. "But not for long," he said. "Not if we make it to the castle in the burning lake before the Eve of Sambain."

Yolette nodded. "If we are successful there," she said, "we should all be in a better place soon."

"Well, at least another place," Nelda said. "Let's hope it's better."

CHAPTER 15

The underground empire created by Lord Vidor for his evil purposes would now, however briefly, be ruled by Sparkle.

Seeing her concern for the inhabitants, Erg and Trog alike, Bret could not bring himself to tell her the real reason he and his companions could not stay. He could not tell her they were on a mission to destroy the evil sorcerer that lived in the castle in the lake of fire. Nor could they tell her that if successful, not only he, but also the entire shadow world he controlled would be obliterated, including her small portion of it. He would not shatter Sparkle's dream for a better life now that the despot, Lord Vidor, was no more. And so, to avoid unnecessary explanations, Bret said only that they had pressing business outside that should be attended to without delay.

In gratitude for his help in freeing her land from the tyrant, Sparkle did not press for details, but agreed to lead him and the others out of the caverns into open country. Tired from their recent ordeal they decided to leave immediately after the next rest period.

* * * * *

Anora, Nelda, and Yolette shared a room while Bret and Sergeant Carney occupied the one next door. The few remaining members of Carney's command slept in a large room down the hall.

Bret lay on one of the beds. He knew that after the rest period he would need his strength for walking and should get some rest. But try as he would, sleep would not come.

Finally he sat up in bed and leaned back on his pillow. Casually, he glanced at the other bed nearby. Sergeant Carney was also sitting up, wide-awake. Hearing the rustle of Bret's covers, he turned to him.

"Can't you sleep either?" he asked.

"No," Bret said. "Guess I'm too wound up about leaving here tomorrow. If we don't get to the castle by the Eve of Sambain everything we've done will be for nothing. And we've lost too much time already."

Carney threw back the covers, got out of bed, and walked to a chair alongside Bret's bed. With a weary groan he sank into it and looked at Bret.

"You know," the sergeant said, "I've been thinking about this mission you have."

Bret nodded. "And what have you decided?" he asked.

Carney shifted uneasily in his chair. "Well," he began, "not to put too fine a point on it, but any man who knows me will tell you I'm not one to shirk my duty."

Bret looked knowingly at the sergeant. "You want to stay here, don't you?" he asked.

Carney twirled his mustache in thought and looked into space. "It comes down to more than just what I want," he said. "Rightly speaking, I believe I and what's left of my command would be more of a liability than a help in what you plan to do."

"How so?"

"You'll have enough trouble talking yourself and the three women into that boat to cross the lake of fire. How would you explain my men and me? No warlock would be traveling with that big an entourage. And the blokes tending the boats would know that."

Bret nodded. "You have a valid point," he agreed.

"And since we'd be of no help to you, whatever time my men and I have left may as well be spent here as anywhere else."

Bret smiled. "I think you've taken a liking to Sparkle," he said.

Sergeant Carney grinned. "You saw through me, didn't you?" he asked. "Well, I'll admit it, I do fancy the little pixy." He shrugged his shoulders. "And besides," he went on, "I lost five more of my men in the battle with Lord Vidor's guards. That leaves only eight lads and me." Carney gazed into space, his eyes tearing up. "Out of a whole battalion we're all that's left."

Bret put a friendly hand on Sergeant Carney's shoulder. "You and your men have earned a rest," he said. "Better for all concerned if you stay with Sparkle."

"I'll do that. And thanks for understanding."

"Nothing to understand," Bret returned. "Like you said, you'd be more of a hindrance than a help."

"Then it's settled," Carney said. A smile of satisfaction spread across his face. Then, just as quickly, it disappeared and he cleared his throat nervously. "About that remark I passed when we first met," he said apologetically. "You know, about writing being a less than manly profession?" Bret nodded. "Well," Carney continued, "I was clearly wrong in my opinion."

"No need to apologize," Bret told him with a chuckle. "Even some people in my own family think I'm a writer only because I can't get a real job."

Sergeant Carney laughed. "Would you believe many a bloke has the same opinion about me? Believe it or not, where I come from, professional soldiers aren't exactly revered in some circles of polite society." Carney laughed again, and, after a short pause, continued in a serious tone. "Since it's not likely we'll be meeting again I want to tell you something. The way you handled yourself in battle made me sorry for saying what I did. I can tell you, there's no man I'd rather have by my side in a fight."

Bret smiled. "Thanks," he said. "You're no slouch yourself when it comes to that."

Carney walked back to the bed and lay down. "I hate good-byes," he said. "So, if you don't mind, I won't see you off. I'll just say good luck, and God-speed."

* * * * *

Following the rest period Bret and the women were up and ready to go. He told them of Sergeant Carney's decision not to leave. They were disappointed but had to agree with his reasoning. Their departure would be one of mixed feelings. They were anxious to get on with their mission. But they would miss the sergeant and his gruff manner.

* * * * *

Bret and the women, now dressed in the clothing they arrived in, met Sparkle in the grand gallery. With outstretched arms and a broad smile she approached the group. Then the smile turned to a look of bewilderment as her pixy-like eyes widened questioningly.

"And where is the sergeant and his men?" she asked.

"He's decided to accept your kind invitation and stay," Bret told her.

Sparkle's smile returned and a happy twinkle came to her eyes. ""Good," she said. "I'll welcome the opportunity to get to know him better." She touched the medallion around her neck. "Shall we be on our way?" she asked. "It's some distance to the outside."

* * * * *

With the power of the medallion creating mysterious passages in solid rock Sparkle led Bret and the women from the inner kingdom to the tunnel on the outlying area. As they progressed the passage slowly changed from well-lighted corridors to dingy rock faced burrows.

* * * * *

At length Sparkle halted at a heavy wooden door. On either side metal rings in the rock wall held flaming torches. She took one down and turned to the others.

"Beyond this portal," she said, "we must rely on torchlight."

* * * * *

For what seemed like an endless trek, Sparkle led Bret, Anora, Nelda, and Yolette through domed grottos and connecting corridors. Little was said as the small party moved along, Sparkle in the lead, holding the torch that lit the way.

* * * * *

At length the travelers saw a faint gray light filling the tunnel ahead. As they rounded a slight bend in the passage they saw the mouth of the cave before them. They were nearly out of the mountain into open country.

Quickening their pace the party soon reached the opening. With mixed emotions, Bret and the women turned to Sparkle. Bret took her tiny hand in his and gazed into her upturned face. Although she smiled, her big, innocent eyes were beginning to fill with tears. Bret leaned down and kissed her gently on the forehead.

"Thank you," he said softly. "We'll never forget you."

Anora put her arm around Sparkle's shoulder. "We certainly won't," she said.

Nelda and Yolette conveyed their thanks to Sparkle with a broad smile. With misty, pixy eyes she slowly scanned the faces of Bret and his friends, then raised her arm in a signal of farewell, and turned and walked away. Her small body was soon enveloped by the darkness of the tunnel as it overpowered the meager flame of the torch.

* * * * *

Stepping from the cavern Bret and the women stood silently looking out over the gloomy, foreboding vista.

A few feet from where they stood, a narrow, rocky road snaked its way upward through the mountain pass to disappear into swirling fog.

Directly across the road, barely visible through the mist, was a marshy field strewn with megaliths. Cracked, tilted, and stained by centuries of wind and rain they stood like ghostly sentinels, ground fog swirling about their base as it crept across the land.

Bret looked at the stone monuments. "Those things give me the willies," he said. "They remind me of a graveyard. They're so forlorn looking, cold and lifeless."

"Oh, I don't know," Nelda said. "When I was a child my family often went on holiday to Brittany. There are a lot of them on the heath there. Erected over four thousand years ago, I'm told. I sort of took a liking to them."

Bret smiled. "Well," he said, "to each his own. Personally, I prefer a vacation site with a little more sunshine. Like the Grand Canyon, for instance."

"Where?" Nelda asked.

"Never mind. I don't think Europeans would have heard of it in your day. Right now we better get started. We have no idea how much more time we have till the Eve of Sambain."

Bret, Anora, Nelda, and Yolette walked to the edge of the road. Then, silently, they started off in the direction of the waxing moon. The road took them upward and through a pass where it ran along the side of the mountain overlooking a deep valley. Beyond, the river snaked its way through the canyon; a sheer cliff shot upward, its summit lost in the clouds.

* * * * *

After several hours Bret and his companions topped the crest of a small hill. Here the road led downward to a rocky plateau. In the distance, where the tableland began sloping toward the foothills, the lights of a small hamlet could be seen.

* * * * *

As they drew nearer the wanderers could make out a high wall enclosing the settlement. Here the road they were traveling came to a fork. One spur, the wider of the two trails, apparently the most used, skirted the village and dropped down into the foothills. The other, narrower and choked with brush, led to the hamlet's front gate.

Bret turned to his companions. "Well, ladies," he asked, "which road? Shall we go on or stop for awhile?"

"I'm awfully tired," Yolette confessed. "And maybe someone there can tell us how far it is to the castle in the burning lake."

"And," Anora added, "we can probably find out how much longer it is to the Eve of Sambain."

"Good idea," Bret agreed. "We don't want to show up at the castle too soon and have to mingle with the others. I don't think I could carry off this masquerade for long among real warlocks. We should get there just before the reckoning. And while the others are having their little game of demonic mayhem we'll search for the grimoire and destroy it. But we'll have to be fast. Get in, do the deed, and get out before anyone catches on."

"Then it's decided," Nelda said. "We spend the coming rest period within the walls of the village."

Bret and the women left the main road and headed toward the settlement. No sooner had they started on the narrow, weed-choked trail than a cold wind rose at their backs. The closer they drew to the village the more bone chilling and raw the cold became. It was as though the walled city and its approaches lay under a cloak of evil, the devil's own icy fingers clawing at the flesh of unwary travelers as they approached. Within the city the light of campfires could be seen, causing Bret and his friends to quicken their pace.

CHAPTER 16

Although a tall rock bulwark surrounded the city, as Bret and his companions drew nearer they were surprised to see there was no gate. Instead, the trail led to an opening in the wall flanked by two huge rectangular rocks supporting a massive capstone. It struck Bret as odd that a walled city would have no portal to control entry, but the numbing cold and the cheery glow of the fires within the village swept away any caution. Quickly he, Anora, Nelda, and Yolette passed through the gateway and headed for the nearest bonfire. As they hurried across a courtyard strewn with rocks they felt a rising wind on their backs as though some unseen power was forcing them onward.

The stooped figures huddled around the fire, dressed in dark, hooded robes, moved closer together to make room for Bret and his companions in the circle. Except for that, they gave no greeting or acknowledgement of their presence, nor did they turn to look at them.

In the orange glow of the fire Bret surveyed his surroundings. The shelters lining the narrow dirt streets were stone, but not built in the usual manner of rock and mortar. The walls were giant blocks of stone shoved together to form rectangular structures. Most were merely windbreaks, having no roofs. A few smaller ones were covered with thick stone slabs. There were no windows in the rough quarried stone walls and the crudely chiseled openings leading into the shelters had no doors.

As Bret and the women held their palms to the fire there was the initial pleasure of warmth, then a sickening stench of sulfur belched from the burning wood. Bret and the women backed away a few steps, turned their heads from the fire and took several deep breaths. The others at the fire made no effort to move. One of the figures turned to Bret and spoke, his voice coming in short, wheezing bursts.

"The brimstone is in the wood," he said. "But it's the only thing we are allowed to have that will burn."

"After you've been here awhile," said another, "you'll become accustomed to it. You'll gladly tolerate the odor in return for warmth."

Bret and the women returned to the fire. "Does this place have a name?" Bret asked the man standing next to him. He really didn't care whether it did or not. He only wanted to initiate a conversation and, in time, ask several questions of importance to him and his friends.

"This place has no name," the man in the tattered robe said. "At least not in the minds of those imprisoned here."

"Imprisoned?" Bret questioned. "But the village is wide open. You can leave any time you want."

"No, my hapless friend. No one can leave."

"Why not? There's no gate. Only an open passage through the wall."

"A clever ploy to entice unwary travelers inside. It's easy to enter here, but impossible to leave."

"Why?" Bret asked. "You only have to walk away."

"Once you enter here the mark of Torak is upon you. And Torak jealously guards his property." The man looked at the women and shook his head. "You will be cruelly used," he continued in a feeble voice betraying a sickening hopelessness. "Torak is a veritable satyr with an insatiable appetite for debauchery." The hooded figure shook his head again. "No woman here escapes his cruel usage," he said.

"We'll just bloody well see about that," Nelda snapped, gripping the handle of the dagger in her belt. "I'll be the first to admit I enjoy a good humping now and then myself. But I'll choose the bloke. And nobody uses me."

"Here," the man said, "I'm afraid you'll have no choice. But it's all beyond your control now. You have unwittingly entered Torak's kingdom, as we all did."

Bret smiled. "And you think you can't leave?" he asked. "Who is this Torak anyway that he wields such power?"

"He makes no effort to hide his previous existence. In fact, rarely misses an opportunity to boast of it. When he was a young man, Morgan le Fay schooled him in the black arts. He spent many years in her service, both as pupil and paramour.

"He boasts that she preferred him to visit her bed rather than another or her pupils, her brother's bastard son, Modred. Modred, it seems, a most vile person in his own right, had not the stomach for the depraved acts Morgan le Fay demanded of a lover. Torak, on the other hand, reveled in them.

"With the death of the king, le Fay's brother, on the embattled shore of Britain the kingdom was overrun. With most of the army in the field, or dead, the castle was practically defenseless. The invading army sacked it and killed all inside, including Torak."

"Now hold on there," Bret said with a skeptical smile on his lips. "Are you talking about King Arthur and the other characters associated with the legend?" The man nodded. "Are you saying they really existed?" Again the man nodded.

"I was a young squire, present at the fall of the castle," he said. "Being in training for knighthood, I took part in the battle. But I'm afraid I was no match for seasoned warriors."

For an instant Bret pursed his lips in thought, then murmured, "Well, why the hell not?" He shook his head. "I always thought King Arthur was s fictional character, the stuff fairy tales are made of. But, a short time ago I wouldn't have believed this shadow world existed either. I guess that just goes to show that just because an idea is popular and prevalent doesn't, necessarily, make it so."

"True," Anora agreed. "The truths of today aren't always the same as those of tomorrow."

Bret rubbed his chin and chuckled. "The earth isn't the center of the universe," he mused in a soft, almost inaudible tone. "And it isn't flat either."

"What did you say?" Yolette asked.

"Oh, nothing," Bret said. "I just remembered something. When my father went to school the scientists of the day had everything wrapped up in a neat package. Every known substance, whether animal, vegetable, or mineral, was composed of one or more of 92 elements. That was all there was, nothing more was possible." Bret smiled. "That idea was proven to be false in my father's lifetime."

True," Yolette said, "scientific facts are of the most fleeting. The alchemists of my day believed all things were composed of four basic elements – earth, air, fire, and water. The concept of even 92 would have been mind-boggling to them."

"I know nothing of these elements," Nelda said. "But it seems that what is fact to one man may not be so to another. And some truths have, apparently, taken on the aura of fable with the passing of time."

"Would that Torak and his evil powers were but fable," the man said, his voice cracking with despair. "But, alas, he exists. And he controls the village and all within its walls.

"Some have dared to leave when his minions were not watching. But their freedom was brief. They were hunted down and returned." The man wrung his hands and shuddered. "Torak was diabolically creative in their punishment," he said. "Those who died were treated kindly compared to the fate of others."

"Where is this Torak?" Bret asked.

"He has gone to the lake of fire to confer with his present mentor. He does so quite regularly. And for that, we are grateful. It gives us a brief respite from his torment." The man shook his head. "There was a time long ago," he said, "that we held hope he may not return from one of these trips, deciding, instead, to stay with his master and mentor. But he always comes back."

"I see. And when he goes he leaves his bully boys behind to keep things in line for him, doesn't he?"

"His personal guards are ever among us, yes."

Bret smiled. "That would be standard practice for someone like him," he said. After a moment of silence, he asked, "Would you mind answering a few questions?"

"What sort of questions?"

"How many rest periods till the Eve of Sambain?"

Again the man shuddered. "We look forward to that time with dread," he said. "Torak always spends it in the castle of his mentor and returns even crueler than before. It's now only four rest periods away."

"And how far is this lake of fire from here?"

"It's said it lies only one rest period's walk away."

"On the road just outside the city?"

The man nodded. "But why would you want to go there?" he asked. Then he straightened and backed away from the fire. "You are a wizard!" he shrieked in a voice fraught with fear. "You journey there for the reckoning!"

"Yes," Bret said. "But there's no need for you to be scared of me. I mean you no harm."

The others in the circle began backing away. "Maybe not," the man said, looking around uneasily, "but should I be found in your company by Torak's men I would be punished." The man shook his head dejectedly. "True," he said, "my present existence here is, at best, miserable. But if he wanted to, Torak could make it even more intolerable."

"Why would he?" Bret asked, trying to allay the man's fears.

"Because," he whispered, "Torak holds a favored place with the all seeing, all knowing evil one who lives in the lake of fire. Any other wizard who seeks to replace him in that position at the reckoning is his enemy. And anyone in their company is, by association, also his enemy."

"Then we'll not endanger you and your brave friends by sharing your fire," Bret said, sarcasm in his voice. "We'll find our own place."

"Or maybe we should just get out of here," Anora said. "We can rest just as well on the trail."

"Better," Nelda said. "At least there it won't be so beastly cold."

"I agree," Yolette said. "This is a baneful place. It reeks of depravity and evil."

Suddenly the wind shifted, bending the flames of the bonfire toward Bret and the women. As the orange tongues of fire leaped and danced and the wood crackled the scent of death and decay permeated the already foul air.

"Before you try to leave this place," the hooded man said, "you would do well to realized the consequences of failure."

The man raised his arm and the firelight played across the back of his emaciated hand, covered with oozing lesions. With a bony finger he pointed beyond the fire. Then, with a weary groan, he stooped and picked up a firebrand. His hand slightly trembling, he thrust it toward Bret.

"Take this," he said, "and go see for yourself."

Bret led the women to where the man had pointed. As they left the circle of light, in the distance, they saw several dark mounds. Even though the sweet, sickening odor was nearly overpowering, Bret held the torch high and continued walking toward the mounds. Although nearly gagging from the stench, Anora, Nelda, and Yolette stayed by his side.

* * * * *

When he and the women were near enough for the torchlight to illuminate the mounds they stopped, for a moment transfixed by the grisly sight. Involuntarily grunting sounds of disgust escaped their lips. In the flickering light of the torch they could see the mounds were, in fact, heaps of putrefying human corpses.

They had been stripped naked and disemboweled. The bodies, in various stages of decay, lay intertwined, their entrails strewn about like nests of sleeping, gray snakes. Small vermin, their beady eyes reflected in the light of the torch, scurrying around and over the reeking piles of rotting cadavers.

"Those are some of the ones who tried," the hooded man called, his voice sharp and clear on the icy air.

* * * * *

Bret and the women returned to join the circle of figures huddled around the bonfire.

"As I told you," the man said, "it's useless to think of leaving here. None in this citadel of the damned has ever passed through the gate to freedom for long." The man threw back his hood. His ashen face was deeply furrowed and a few tufts of gray hair clung to his wrinkled scalp. "When first I wandered into this accursed place," he said in a low, choking voice, "I, too, entertained thoughts of escape." He waved his arm in the direction of the bodies piled nearby. "Most of those on that moldering heap over there were my friends," he said. "Or as close to friends as one can come in this hellish spot. A long time ago, when Torak was on one of his frequent absences, I foolishly led them through the gate to what I believed would be freedom."

The man fell silent for a moment and stared blankly into space. Then, with a catch in his voice, he went on.

"We had gone only a few hundred yards when we were set upon by hordes of Torak's hairy beasts. With clubs they beat us into bloody submission and dragged us back here for punishment." Again the man looked in the direction of the mounds of putrefying corpses, then at Bret. "I was not treated as kindly as they," he said. "I wish I could join them instead of enduring the punishment dealt me by Torak."

"What could be worse than what he did to your friends?" Bret asked.

The man's sunken eyes filled with tears. Then, he ripped open his robe exposing a chest riddled with seeping, open wounds and blotches of maggot ridden rotting flesh. The women turned away at the sudden impact of nauseating odor while Bret stared in disbelief.

"I was condemned to forever walk the streets of this accursed village a hideous paradox," the man sobbed. "I breathe, I feel cold and hunger, yet I am nothing more than a walking, rotting corpse, barely able to abide the stench of my own body."

"O.K., that's it," Bret said. "Let's get out of here and back on the main trail. We have to get to the castle in the lake of fire."

"Good idea," Nelda said. "But I just had the most disturbing thought."

"What's that?" Bret asked.

"Wouldn't you agree this Torak is about as evil a person as anyone could imagine?" Bret, Anora, and Yolette nodded. "Well, has it occurred to you," Nelda continued, "that he, as vile as he is, is subservient to, and probably afraid of the wizard that lives in the lake of fire?"

"I see what you mean," Bret said. "And he's the one we'll be going up against. But it doesn't change anything. Besides, after seeing this place I'm more anxious than ever to get on with it. So let's get moving."

* * * * *

When Bret and his friends neared the stone portal, four dark figures stepped from the shadows into their path. Had they not been scantily dressed in uniforms of a sort, in the flickering light of the campfires, they could have been mistaken for large apes. Their black eyes glared at Bret and the women from beneath Neanderthal brows. These figures, apparently Torak's gatekeepers, stood slightly stooped and their bodies were extremely hairy. This covering apparently insulated them against the elements, as in spite of the bone chilling cold they wore only leather codpieces and harness across their chest. They carried huge clubs in their gnarled hands.

Bret looked at the women, then at the open gate, only yards away, then back to Torak's guards as they advanced.

CHAPTER 17

On the cold, windswept courtyard, only yards from the wall, with its open passage leading from the city, Bret and his friends faced Torak's guards. Menacingly, the ape-like creatures moved slowly toward them at a lumbering gait, raising their gnarled clubs as they advanced.

"What now?" Anora asked. "We'll never get around these guards."

Bret's hand flashed to the handle of the sword that hung from his left hip.

"Then we'll have to go through them," he said. "We've come too far to be stopped now."

"Right you are," Nelda said, her hand encircling the handle of the dagger tucked in her belt. "We'll bloody well go through them or join those poor devils rotting away by the fence over there." With a snort of defiance, she tossed her head in the direction of the mound of human decay beyond the bonfire.

"They don't look to me like they'd be very quick on their feet," Bret said. "And we'll have the element of surprise on our side, in a way. I don't think they've ever gone up against anyone that fought back. They're probably used to beating helpless, scared victims with those clubs. With a little footwork we should be able to avoid them."

"I hope you're right," Nelda said. "But in any case, we'll make a fight of it." Slowly she drew her dagger. In the dismal constant twilight that hung over the city her subtle movement went unnoticed by the guards. Anora and Yolette slowly sank to the ground. The guards snickered and looked at each other in amusement. But the women were not cowering in fear as they thought. Unnoticed by the advancing sentinels Anora and Yolette each picked up a heavy rock.

"I'll not be taken either," Yolette vowed. She rose and stood beside Bret and Nelda.

"Nor I," Anora said, straightening and stepping to Yolette's side.

"All right then," Bret said softly, "let's go for it. They're big but they move slow and don't look very bright. If we take them by surprise we should be able to outmaneuver them. When I make my play back me as best you can."

The guards were now within a few feet of Bret and his friends. It was obvious Torak's ape-like minions were expecting no resistance. They advanced not in a battle rank but in a ragged formation. One, the largest of the four, walked in the lead while the others followed in a staggered line, three abreast.

When the leader was within three feet of him Bret drew his cutlass and lunged forward. Before the startled guard could raise his club the blade sank into his hairy chest At the same instant Nelda sprang forward, thrusting her dagger into the throat of another sentry standing to the left of the leader. He sank to the ground, strangling on his own blood.

Bret had barely time to withdraw his blade from the chest of his fallen foe when the other two sprang forward. The one slightly in the forefront swung his club in a looping downward chop. Bret easily avoided the heavy cudgel and it hit the ground with a thud. Before the hairy beast could recover Bret plunged the cutlass into his side. The creature let out a scream, dropped his club, and fell to his knees. Bret jerked the blade free and quickly jabbed the point into the wounded guard's throat. With a contemptuous grunt, he twisted the blade, then put his foot on the guard's chest and sent him tumbling backward, his lifeblood gushing from his severed jugular.

Nelda faced the last guard. With a grunt of mounting rage, the hairy creature swung his club. Nelda ducked under the blow and sprang forward, her dagger flashing upward toward the creature's throat. But before the blade could reach its mark the guard grabbed her wrist. Snarling, he dropped his club, and, with his other hand, jerked her to his chest. The crushing, vise-like grip applied to her waist forced Nelda to drop the dagger. Releasing her wrist, he threw his hairy arms around her waist. A sharp yelp of pain escaped her lips as he crushed her to his chest in a paralyzing bearhug. Snarling vengefully, he lifted her off the ground and spun her around, foolishly turning his back to the others. He jostled her up and down, tightening his grip as she dangled helplessly like a rag doll.

Seeing Nelda in trouble, Anora and Yolette sprang into action. Anora smashed the enraged creature in the spine with the rock. At the same time Yolette brought hers crashing down on his head. The beast released his grip on Nelda, dropped her to the ground, and turned to face the two women, his face livid with anger. Swiftly Nelda picked up her dagger from the ground and thrust it into the guard's back. For an instant, he stood on shaky legs glaring at Anora and Yolette. Then, he pitched forward, dead.

Bret turned to the women. "Is anyone hurt?" he asked.

"No," Nelda said. "I may be a little sore for a day or so from that bearhug, but noting serious."

"I'm fine," Anora said as she dropped the rock she still held in her hand.

With eyes downcast Yolette gazed at the bloody rock still in her small, delicate hand. Then she pitched it to the ground and looked at Bret.

"I'm unhurt as well," she said softly. A subtle, nervous smile spread across her face. "In fact," she added, "it's a little embarrassing, but I feel a strange exhilaration. After so long a victim it felt good to strike back for a change."

"Don't be embarrassed," Nelda said. "No one wants to be the victim. And, sooner or later, everyone will fight back when they have a chance."

Bret smiled admiringly at his three companions. "You all did good," he said. He slid the cutlass back into the scabbard at his waist and put his hand on Yolette's shoulder.

"For such a little girl," he said, "you got a lot of fight in you."

Yolette pressed close to Bret and slipped her arm around his waist. With a coquettish smile she looked up into his eyes.

"I may be little," she said, "but I'm not a girl. In my world I was considered a full grown woman."

The steady stare of Yolette's dark brown eyes made Bret a little uncomfortable. Until now he had thought of her as an adolescent. But suddenly, with her statement, he saw her in a whole different light.

Damn, Bret thought, this could get awkward. With a nervous smile he tore his gaze from hers and looked across the courtyard, toward the fire where they had recently stood. The figures there were still huddled around the flames. Fearfully, they had ignored the struggle and even now dared not look in the direction of Bret and his companions, much less the slain guards. Bret shook his head. Torak sure has these poor devils buffaloed, he thought. They're trying so hard to pretend they never saw the fight for fear they might be implicated in some way. He turned back to Anora, Nelda, and Yolette.

"Ladies," he said, "I suggest we get out of here before more of those apes show up."

"I agree," Nelda said. "We should get as far away as possible. Sooner or later more of those hairy blokes are going to stumble onto their pals here and decide to take out after us."

"And if the castle is only one rest period's walk away, as we were told," Bret reasoned, "we should make it there before anyone catches up to us."

As he started toward the portal the women fell in beside him. Together the four exited the cursed city and started toward the main road they had left only a short time ago.

* * * * *

When Bret and the woman walked through the gateway a blast of cold wind nearly swept them off their feet. Doggedly, they leaned into the gale, and, with their heads down, trudged toward the fork in the road.

* * * * *

Once back on the main road the wind subsided. With an apprehensive last look at the walled city, Bret and the women turned and walked toward the waxing moon.

A few hundred yards ahead the meandering road led them downward into a shallow valley choked with brush. The pathway narrowed till it was barely wide enough for one person to walk between the prickly vegetation crowding in on both sides.

Bret looked back over his shoulder. "So far, so good," he said. "I don't think anyone's following us. At least not very close behind."

"Those hairy creatures didn't seem too smart to me," Nelda said. "Even if they've found the ones we killed, without Torak to tell them what to do, they may be too stupid to get organized and come after us."

"It would be comforting to believe that," Yolette said. "But, somehow, I doubt it."

Nelda grinned. "You're right, of course," she admitted. "Even I don't believe that. Guess I was just whistling past the graveyard, so to speak."

"I'm getting pretty tired," Anora said. "We have plenty of time to reach the castle before the Eve of Sambain, and, apparently, there isn't anyone following us as yet. So, do you think we could rest a bit?"

"I could do with some rest too," Nelda said.

"And I too," Yolette said with a weary smile.

"O.K.," Bret agreed. "We have time. And, besides, we want to get to the castle as rested and alert as possible. We'll get off the road into the brush. It's so thick no one could spot us there even if they walked right past us."

* * * * *

A few yards off the pathway, through a thick stand of brush, was a small clearing large enough to accommodate the weary travelers. The grassy ground was canopied by long branches of the surrounding trees, making detection from the nearby hills unlikely.

Bret surveyed the shadowy area. "Well, ladies," he said, "we might as well get some rest. If what we were told in the village back there is true the lake of fire isn't too far from here. We should be able to make it there, bright eyed and bushy tailed, with plenty of time to spare."

Nelda stretched and yawned. "Right on," she said. "I could do with a bit of a snooze."

Bret and his friends lay on the ground. Although the grass beneath his back was damp, he soon drifted of into a light sleep.

* * * * *

Bret awoke to find Yolette lying by his side, her head resting in the hollow of his shoulder. Her delicate features were bathed in the soft, eternal twilight of the waxing moon and her dark brown eyes were filled with a look of sad longing. A sudden erotic urge welled up within him, but was quickly dispelled by a feeling of guilt. She's only a child, he told himself. Then he remembered what she had said. In her time she would be considered a full-grown woman. She moaned softly and snuggled closer. The erotic feeling began returning, and, this time, he made no effort to dispel it. Instinctively he reached across and began to caress her hair.

"Please don't think of me as shameless," she said softly. Bret gave no reply, but continued to stroke her hair and she snuggled closer to him. "I'll leave if you want me to," she said, a sadness in her voice.

Bret gently stroked her cheek. "Only if you want to," he said in a soft whisper.

Yolette put her arm across his chest. "Our time is short," she said. "Soon all that we now know will be gone. I'm sure that what awaits us will be better. But still . . ." Yolette put her lips to Bret's ear and continued to whisper. "It may seem shameless of me, but I don't want to pass from this existence feeling cheated of the things other women have enjoyed. All that I have known of men is cruelty at the hands of my inquisitor, Gano Cuvier."

Bret gave Yolette a firm, sympathetic hug. "Don't judge all men by him," he said. "Most of us are gentle with women, and treat them with kindness."

"So Anora and Nelda have told me," Yolette said, sadness in her voice. "I feel a great void in my life for never having felt a man's tender touch. I was deprived of that experience by a cruel fate." Yolette snuggled even closer.

"I've been wanting to tell you," she said, "since first we met, I've had a certain fondness for you." Yolette smiled and closed her eyes in embarrassment. "Of late," she went on almost in a whisper, "the feeling has changed. Being with you has roused urges within me I thought I would never feel." After a brief silence Yolette slipped her leg over his and pressed her pelvis to his thigh. Slowly, she began moving her hips in a gentle rotating motion. "Please don't think of me as shameless," she whispered, "but I want to experience what other women have known before we reach the burning lake and the joy is lost to me forever." She opened her eyes, now misty with desire.

Bret rolled over and kissed her gently, softly, their lips barely touching. Gently, she slipped her hand behind Bret's head and pulled him to her, returning the kiss with a passionate hunger. Their lips united in a long, deep kiss, she snuggled closer to him.

Deftly, Bret unbuttoned her blouse and cupped her petite breast in his hand. His lips still on hers, he gently stroked it, the palm of his hand teasing and exciting her erect nipple. Then he moved his mouth from hers to kiss her other breast.

Her eyes closed, Yolette relished each new sensation, foreign as they were, as they came stealing into her body. Then she felt the jolting, burning rush of passion sweep over her as he took the nipple in his mouth and began gently sucking it. She felt a tingling sensation of warmth in her nipple as though a tiny fire had been kindled. Rapidly the sensation spread through her body and she surrendered to the warmth, her breasts heaving, her hips slowly gyrating.

Now completely consumed with desire, Yolette's breath came in short, passionate gasps as Bret gently raised her skirt and moved between her legs.

"I don't want to hurt you," he whispered as he slowly began to enter her. "Tell me if it hurts and I'll stop."

With the first feeling of penetration the pent-up passion and desires of centuries suddenly washed over her body like a crashing flow of molting lava rushing down a slope of an exploding volcano. A low moan escaped her parted lips as she grabbed him by the buttocks and pulled him forward, burying him to the hilt within her.

Her lips close to his ear, her hot breath fueling his desire, she replied in a throaty whisper, "Don't worry about hurting me." She slid her hands up his back and wrapped her arms around his shoulders. With another passionate moan she crushed him to her breast. "I'm not a child," she breathed. "I'm a woman."

* * * * *

When Bret awoke Anora and Nelda were already up. Smiling, they looked down at him, Yolette snuggling in his arms.

"Are you two going to sleep right through to the next rest period?" Anora asked.

"Not that we're in that much of a hurry," Nelda said. "I figure we have about three more rest periods till the Eve of Sambain."

Bret got to his feet and helped Yolette up. "If that person back there in the walled city was right," he said. "But he could be wrong."

Nelda smiled knowingly as she looked at Yolette then Bret. "Maybe now you aren't so anxious to get to the castle in the burning lake," she chided.

Anora smiled at Yolette who blushed and looked down at her feet. "From the look on your face," she said, "I'd say you didn't spend the last rest period getting much rest. And I'm sure you'd like to continue not getting much rest. Are you sure you want to do away with things as they are?"

Before Bret could answer, Yolette spoke up. "Yes," she replied. She looked at Bret and smiled, then looked back to Anora. "I'll not deny it was a most pleasurable experience," she told her. "But there are too many tortured souls here to be selfishly concerned with my own life."

"I suppose," Bret said, "some like Sparkle and Sergeant Carney and others we left back there in the caverns probably don't have it too bad right now. But I'm sure that will change soon if they devil living in the lake of fire is as powerful as he seems to be. But even if that were not so, how can we forget those poor devils in the walled city we just left? That alone makes me even more resolved to go through with our plan."

"Of course, you're right," Nelda said. "But before we get there I'd just like to tell you it's been a pleasure knowing you."

"It's been my pleasure to know all three of you," Bret replied. "You're all something special." He turned toward the edge of the thicket. "I'll never forget any of you," he said. "But we have a job to do, so let's get on with it."

* * * * *

The narrow pathway led to the base of a lofty plateau. Here it widened and gently sloped up along the side of the mountain. The ground on either side of the trail was brush covered and dotted with an occasional boulder. Before reaching the summit the pathway cut back several times, snaking its way to the top.

* * * * *

When Bret and the women neared the mountaintop there was a faint orange glow in the sky. A short time later, when they reached the summit, the source of the glow was evident. For a long moment the four stood silent, looking down from the lofty pinnacle.

From here the road led ever downward. Below, in a valley shrouded in shadows and swirling mist, was the lake of fire.

CHAPTER 18

From the brow of the hill the land sloped gently down to the fiery lake in the valley below. Against the backdrop of eternal twilight the leaping flames cast an eerie glow across the inky water while belching clouds of black, churning smoke into the air.

The flames did not cover the entire surface of the water, but burned only in a wide circle around the island in its center. There, atop the lofty crags, dark and brooding in the pale, somber moonlight sat the stronghold of the evil master of the land. A few yards from where Bret, Anora, Nelda, and Yolette stood, the road leading down disappeared into a dense thicket of brush and gnarled trees.

The steep climb to the tableland had been long and tiring for Bret and his companions. And had their goal not been in sight they would have surrendered to fatigue and rested. But as they stood on the brow of the hill, looking down into the valley, they felt a sudden surge of energy, and a strange force urging them to plunge ahead.

"Well," Bret said, "so far, so good. We can't stop now. It's only a little farther to the lake."

"You think we'll have any trouble getting across?" Anora asked.

"I don't think so," Bret replied. He looked down at the castle perched atop the hill in the center of the burning lake and smiled. "Anyone but a witch or warlock would be crazy to go near that valley, much less the burning lake and castle," he said. "Especially during the reckoning. So the boatman probably won't ask any questions, and ferry anyone across the lake that asks to go."

"I'm sure that's right," Yolette said. "From what I've heard, this reckoning is more than just a gathering of witches and warlocks to display their arcane powers. To the devil living in that castle, it's a way to pick the one that will help him run his evil kingdom. And just so no one gets too comfortable in that job, they have to prove themselves all over again each year."

"And I'm sure he revels in the mayhem they create in the process," Anora said. "I've heard it's quite a long procedure, and rarely do the witches and warlocks expose themselves to danger in the deadly struggle. Not until the very end anyway. Instead, they conjure up their personal spawn from hell to do battle for them. Then they sit back and direct their demons. Sometimes the struggle lasts for days with these abominations from hell ripping and tearing at each other. So, for the evil warlord of the land, the more candidates, the longer and more entertaining the proceedings."

"Since it's the more the merrier," Bret said, "we should be able to get across the lake with no problem."

"True," Yolette agreed. "But once there, if we aren't convincing enough in our rolls and our true purpose is discovered . . . " Yolette's voice trailed off into silence. She didn't have to finish the sentence. They all knew what failure would mean.

"Well, then," Bret said, "we just better damned well not let that happen."

"How do you plan to locate the grimoire?" Anora asked.

"I'm sure the gathering will be a regular bacchanal, a feast of depravity. The castle will be filled with a collection of the vilest characters imaginable. This battle royal isn't due to start till the Eve of Sambain. So, until then, I can imagine what they'll be doing to pass the time. And, unless I miss my guess, they'll have the run of the castle. Except one room, that is. The room where the host of this shindig keeps his book of shadows. And it's bound to be the only one with guards on the door."

"Sounds logical to me," Anora said.

* * * * *

The trail down the sloping side of the mesa was narrow, the thorny underbrush pressing in from both sides. An occasional gnarled tree sat lonely and forlorn amid the undergrowth, its dying limbs reaching across the pathway like bony arms, draped with shrouds of dead moss.

* * * * *

When Bret and his companions emerged from the brush choked pathway onto the lakeshore they were met with a rancid, sickening odor. A few yards ahead six narrow, rickety docks ran out over the black, scummy water. At the approach of each wharf, a torch, lashed to a gnarled post, cast an eerie yellow glow.

Alongside one of the rotting wharves, a ferryman, dressed in a black robe and hood, stood in his boat silently awaiting his next passenger. The black gondola rode high in the water, the human skull decorating its high, pointed prow nodding ghoulishly as the craft rose and fell with the waves lapping against the lakeshore, its side banging rhythmically against the pilings.

Silently, their heads bowed, Bret, Anora, Nelda, and Yolette walked to the waiting gondola and stepped aboard. The boatman took no special note of the four as the craft, under some strange, unseen power, began to move away from shore toward the castle.

* * * * *

Bret and his friends felt the increasing heat as they neared the fiery ring. Now they could hear the roar of the flames, but the gondola's speed never slackened. When the bow of the craft came within inches of the roaring wall of flames, they parted, leaving a narrow waterway. The gondola sailed straight ahead, into the roaring inferno, flames leaping on both sides. But, strangely, inside the gondola Bret and his companions felt no sensation of heat from the crackling walls of fire. In fact, a cold, dank shroud seemed to settle on the craft as it pressed on toward the island in the center of the lake.

* * * * *

When the boat slid silently past the inner wall of the fiery ring the rockbound shore of the island came into view. Rotting docks, similar to those on the lakeshore, jutted out into the murky water. As the gondola approached the island the faint odor of death and decay pervaded the air. The nearer the gondola approached the shore, where torches shed their sparse light on the docks and moss covered mooring posts, the more pronounced the odor became.

* * * * *

As the gondola slid alongside the dock with a hollow thump, in the torchlight Bret and his companions saw large rats scurry down the shoulder-high pilings and run up the rickety wharf toward shore. In their rush some fell into the slimy, flotsam covered water with a soft, muffled splash. With only their heads above the water, they knifed toward shore, leaving a v-shaped ripple in their wake. As they climbed from the water their wet coats revealed gaunt, ferret-like bodies and their beady eyes glinted in the flickering torchlight as they disappeared among the weeds along the muddy bank.

When the gondola came to a stop Bret and the women stepped out onto the dock. Looking back toward the leaping flames of the lake they saw a fine mist began to form above the inferno. As it rose the vapor began to spread, forming a low, flat cloud. Then it settled to the water and began rolling toward the island. Soon Bret and his companions were engulfed in a chilling fog.

With a gnarled hand, the boatman threw back his cowl revealing a cadaverous face and wrinkled baldpate. He breathed a hoarse sigh, and, for the first time, spoke.

"The gathering is complete," he said. "My task is done." He looked upward, toward the castle perched atop the hill, its crumbling ramparts soaring into the dark sky. "So mote it be," he murmured.

"What do you mean?" Bret asked, a slight stammer of surprise in his voice. "It isn't the Eve of Sambain yet is it? I thought it was three more rest periods away."

The boatman turned and looked at Bret with sad, sunken eyes. "For one who hopes to sit by the master's side you are careless in your calculations," he said. "The master has closed the way. No more may enter for the reckoning."

Slowly, silently the gondola edged away from the dock and was soon lost in the rolling mist.

Bret turned to the women. "Looks like that poor devil back at the walled city was confused," he said. "The Eve of Sambain was closer than he thought. We just got in under the wire."

"What?" Anora asked

"Just an expression of my time," Bret said. "It means we barely made it in time. We caught the last boat."

"Let's hope that's the case," Yolette said.

"What do you mean by that?" Nelda asked.

"The evil master up there is said to be able to look into the farthest dark corners of this accursed land." Yolette paused, then went on. "Doesn't it seem a bit odd he stopped the boats right after we arrived?"

"You think he's on to us?" Anora asked. "And he stopped the boats as soon as he knew we were on the island?"

Yolette shook her head. "I don't know," she replied.

"I think you're reading to much into this," Bret said. "We were mistaken about the date and just caught the last boat, that's all." Bret looked up at the dark castle. "But even if what you say is true," he went on, "it doesn't change anything." He looked at the women and added, "At least not for me. I intend to go ahead with our original plan and try to bluff my way into the castle, look for the book of shadows, and get rid of it. But if what Yolette says turns out to be true, there's not a chance. So, if you want to stay here I'll understand."

"What, pack it in now?" Nelda asked incredulously, indignation in her voice. "Not a bit of it. Not on your rosy red keister, mate. I'll have none of that. So don't you get any ideas about beaching me. We all started together, and I, for one, want to be in on the finish." After a slight pause, she added, "Whatever that happens to be."

"Exactly," Anora said. "What have we got to lose?"

"Only the never ending torment," Yolette said. "Even if we are expected, it's better to try than to give up now."

Nelda smiled. "You know," she began, "I really don't fear or even dread the physical abuse any more. I've gotten numb to that, developed a certain detachment. I think I detest the constant boredom the most. But that hasn't been a problem of late." Nelda smiled and touched Bret's hand. "Thank you," she said.

"Believe me," Bret said, "being here with you girls has been a unique experience for me too. It's a lifestyle I never thought I'd experience." Bret turned and looked upward. The craggy outline of the castle shimmered and faded momentarily with the passing of a low cloud. Then it shot back into prominence against the gray sky and pale moonlight. "We better get started," Bret said. "It's still a good walk to the castle. And we don't want to get lost in this damned fog."

Beyond the wharves a flagstone pathway led sharply upward to the main gate of the castle. The swirling fog was thickening; its churning billows gobbling up the meager torchlight like a hungry beast.

* * * * *

As Bret, Anora, Nelda, and Yolette trudged up the pathway toward the castle they soon found themselves above the fog. Now they were able to see tall, thin stone megaliths, carved with strange esoteric symbols, standing along the roadway like silent sentinels on a lonely watch. Farther back from the path, nearly shrouded in darkness, others rose from the dank, moldering grass like huge, crumbling tombstones.

Looking back toward the wharves, they could barely make them out through the mist. The swirling blanket of fog subdued even the light from the leaping orange flames as it spread across the lake. The inferno now seemed to glow like a banked fire in the hearth of a giant furnace.

Suddenly, a chilling wind swept down from the mountaintop. To protect their faces Bret and the women turned their backs to the gale. As the wind whistled past their heads they covered their ears with the palms of their hands. Still they shivered in its icy grip. Then, as suddenly as it rose, the wind died.

"I guess that was our official welcome," Bret said, briskly rubbing his arms.

"Or a warning," Anora said.

"Or maybe just a natural cold breeze," Nelda offered.

"Well," Bret said, "whatever it was has stopped now. So let's get on our way. Maybe it'll be warmer inside the castle.

* * * * *

The road made a slight curve around an outcropping of rocks and ended abruptly at the main entrance to the castle. Bret grasped the huge metal ring on one of the ironclad double wooden gates and brought it down with a thud. Slowly the portal creaked open. As soon as Bret and his friends passed through the opening the gate swung shut with an ominous thud.

* * * * *

The four stood for a moment in the courtyard knowing they would never pass through the gateway again. Within the dark walls of the castle they would find either release from their baneful existence in this hellish land or an eternity of unbearable torment far greater than they had known before.

CHAPTER 19

Inside the gate, Bret and his friends stood for a moment surveying their new surroundings. The ancient stone walls, topped with broken battlements, stood black and ominous against the gray sky. Silhouetted against the somber background, minions of the demonic lord of the manor moved along the ramparts in a silent, eternal vigil. Moss covered stones, fallen from a crumbling turret, lay in the pale moonlight, oozing slime.

The courtyard was overgrown with weeds and strewn with the bones of small animals. Narrow fingers of cold, wispy fog spread across the ground like searching tentacles. The damp air hung heavy with the subtle, yet unmistakable, odor of sulfur mingled with the nauseating smell of decay and stagnate water.

Across the courtyard six well-worn stone steps led to a landing next to the main bulwark of the castle. Atop the rise a heavy wooden door, reinforced with wrought iron straps and large hinges, stood slightly ajar. Above the din of voices in wild revelry coming from the doorway the occasional sound of demonic laughter and shrieks of delight stabbed through the foul air.

Bret and his companions looked cautiously around. Grotesque gargoyles jutted from the stone walls. The torches they held in their claw-like hands cast eerie shadows on their leering faces and bathed the surrounding area in an orange glow. Above these hideous torchbearers the walls were black with soot of centuries. In the shimmering light these blotches glistened like pools of hot, running tar.

Without a word, Bret, Anora, Nelda, and Yolette crossed the courtyard and ascended the stone steps to the door. Slowly, Bret pushed it full open and they stepped through the entrance to stand on a wide stone landing.

* * * * *

Beyond the portal three broad steps led down into the great hall, illuminated by torches held by metal rings in the walls and hundreds of flickering black candles. Dark, ominous shadows danced in the corner of the room, across the vaulted ceiling, and in the four yawning archways where staircases led upward. The room, although cavernous, was crowded and rang with the bedlam of jumbled conversation, often punctuated with cackling laughter and hellish shrieks.

The witches and warlocks assembled milled about, pressing their bodies together as they passed from one to the other. Most of the warlocks wore dark, floor length robes, their faces obscured within hoods. Others wore colorful cassocks and headdresses of animal skin topped with horns. Some of the witches were clad in dark robes and long capes. But the majority was drape in a diaphanous mantle reaching the floor. As they moved among the gathering, their bodies appeared snow-white against the backdrop of dark, cavorting figures.

Bret turned to the women as they nervously surveyed the room. Then he caught their eyes.

"Looks like you ladies are a bit overdressed," he said with an impish twinkle in his eyes. The women smiled and nodded, but gave no reply.

On the floor of the room stood a large stone basin, filled to overflowing with moss choked black water reeking of stagnation. Above this, imbedded in the stone wall, a gargoyle spurted water from its mouth into the basin, making a dull, splattering sound when it struck the slimy flotsam.

When the witches and warlocks, in their milling, passed the reeking fount they scooped up the slimy water in their hands and splashed it on their faces. Some put their cupped hands to their lips and gulped down the putrid liquid with noisy slurping sounds.

Anora put her hand on Yolette's arm and pointed in the direction of the fountain.

"Why are they drinking that slime?" she asked, wrinkling her nose in disgust.

"It's a symbolic gesture associated with the black arts," Yolette said. "To a demonic devotee, drinking the stagnate water is symbolic of their power over death and its black color their devotion to the powers of darkness." Yolette shot a contemptuous glance toward the fountain. "We who practice the white magic of Wicca find it as repulsive as you do," she concluded.

Bret shook his head. "And I thought my fraternity initiation back at college was rough," he said.

On the far end of the hall stood a dais. There, in a throne decorated with human skulls, sat a lean, dark man. The blood-red robe he wore covered him from neck to ankles. Emblazoned on his chest was a goat's head within an inverted, five-pointed star, the commonly recognized symbol of Satan. His long, black hair was pulled back in a ponytail, giving his face a gaunt look and his eyes, beneath bushy, black eyebrows, a curious slant.

Suddenly Yolette grasped Bret's arm. "That man on the throne is Gano Cuvier," she said in a shaky voice.

"Are you sure?" Bret asked.

"I'm not likely to forget him. Not after what he did to me."

Anora, hearing the conversation, looked in the direction of the dais. "That's Perrin Fortier," she said. "He's the devil that posed as a portrait painter to gain access to my husband's estate."

Nelda looked at the man on the dais. "Well," she mused, "that scurvy bilge rat sure gets around. I don't suppose you'd be amazed to know that I knew him as Auburt Guignard, a bar owner in Port-au-Prince."

"Well," Anora said, "we shouldn't be surprised. We knew the same man, known to us by different names, sent us all here. We shouldn't be astonished to find he runs this hellish place."

Nelda smiled. "Right on," she said. "And that will make it even sweeter when we burn his book of shadows and send him back to Satan's hell where he belongs."

On the right side of this man sat another in a smaller throne. He, too, was lean and dark, with long black hair reaching to his shoulders. He wore a long green robe decorated with red astrological symbols. His black skullcap, reaching to his brow in a widow's peak, was cut out to reveal his pointed ears.

"That devil to the right of the head man must be Torak, the ruler of that walled city we passed through," Bret surmised.

"I'm sure he is," Yolette agreed. She looked around cautiously, and turned to the others. "So far," she said in a low voice, "the master of this foul world doesn't seem to be aware that we're here. I'm sure he's probing the minds of everyone, reveling in their hateful thoughts of unleashing their personal demons to tear the others to shreds. He probably hasn't gotten around to us yet. But I'm sure he'll soon sense our presence and our mission."

"Then we better get on with it," Bret suggested. "We better get down on the floor where we won't be so conspicuous. Stay close to me and we'll make our way across the floor to one of those staircases. If we're casual about it no one should even notice us leaving the hall."

Yolette took hold of Bret's arm. "If our purpose here is sensed by him," she said, "he'll have his guards on us in a flash. If that happens, you must separate from us as though you didn't know us. I'm still convinced he can't sense your presence or motives. You'll have to do what must be done alone."

* * * * *

Slowly, Bret and the women descended the staircase and merged with the crowd. Instantly, they were swallowed up by the mob. Swept along by the unruly throng, amid jostling, shoving, and groping, they made their way across the room.

With their backs to the wall, they edged their way toward the nearest staircase. Then, with a cautious glance toward the dais, they stealthily backed into the archway. Once hidden by the shadows, they turned and picked their way silently up the staircase, dimly lit by a pale light drifting down from above.

* * * * *

Standing in the archway of the landing the four looked up and down the deserted corridor.

"Which way?" Nelda asked.

"Pick one, right or left," Bret said.

Yolette put her hand to the talisman around her neck. It was warm to the touch. "I think we should go right," she said.

Bret turned to her. "That's as good a guess as any, I suppose," he said. Yolette smiled and took her hand away from the charm. Bret looked at her with stunned curiosity.

"What is it?" Yolette asked.

"That thing around your neck is shining," he said. "It didn't do that before, did it?"

Yolette looked down at the bauble. "No," she said, "it never has." Again she took it in her hand and a faraway look came to her eyes. "A voice tells me we should go to the right," she said in a soft monotone. Then Yolette smiled. "It's the voice of Madame Sibyla, my mentor," she beamed.

* * * * *

Below, in the great hall, the master rose from his throne and raised his hands above his head. The unholy gathering hushed their chatter and began to chant. Gradually, it rose from a murmur to a resounding roar as the chanting staccato of voices thundered through the chilly air, reverberating from wall to wall and floor to ceiling.

Suddenly, with a wave of his arm the master silenced the crowd. Again he reached skyward, his eyes blazing, a ghoulish grin spreading across his pallid face. Then he spoke in a rumbling voice that cut through the charged air like the slashing of a sword.

"All powerful master," he boomed, "lord of the brimstone depths, show us the path of evil and grant us your favor."

The air crackled with electricity, the stench of sulfur and human decay pervaded the atmosphere to settle like a rotting shroud on the assembled wizards and their captive demons.

An unnatural, cold wind rose from nowhere, howling through the room like millions of screaming tormented souls. Yet, above the resounding discord, the rumble of thunder could be heard. It rolled and crashed like the hellish laughter of the damned. And instantly all present knew it was the master's signal for the havoc to begin.

CHAPTER 20

The tension in the room mounted as the sorcerers marshaled their powers, awakening the private demons within them for the coming battle. The howling of the wind rose to a deafening crescendo and lightning crackled, sending blue flames playing over the vaulted ceiling, a sign that the demons were ready, their malevolent powers at their peak. Then, as suddenly as it had risen, the howling wind died into a chilling dirge of silence.

Metamorphosing from their masters, hosts of demons rose into the air weaving menacingly above them. Then, as if by silent commands, they sprang at each other, streaking through the great hall, levitating amidst the crackling bolts of lightning raining from the ceiling. Like hungry wolves they fell upon each other, ripping and tearing with their claws and teeth.

* * * * *

Upstairs, Bret and the women picked their way along a dimly lit corridor. The uproar of the battle raging below was not completely absorbed by the thick stone walls, and they could hear the shrieks and screams of the vanquished demons being ripped to bits in the hellish struggle.

"Sounds like the war has started," Bret said.

"Yes," Yolette agreed. "It'll probably go on for several hours. But, just in case it doesn't, we better find the book soon."

"What does that voice tell you?" Bret asked. "Are we going in the right direction?"

"I haven't heard it since we started. So I suppose we must be on the right track."

* * * * *

At length Bret and the women came to a turn in the hallway. Cautiously, he peered around the corner, then turned back to the women, a smile on his face.

"That must be it," he said. "There are two guards standing in front of a door, about twenty feet ahead."

"Only two?" Nelda quipped. "This should be easy."

"I don't think they're going to be pushovers. I recognize the hairy, warthog faces with the beady eyes and tusks. They're part of the gang that terrorizes the countryside. The ones you call tormentors." Bret stole another glance around the corner. "They're pretty well armed," he said. "They're both carrying swords. One has a javelin, and the other is holding a battle-axe across his chest, cradling it in his left arm."

"What would you suggest?" Nelda asked, drawing her dagger from her belt. "A straightforward, head-on attack? Or something more subtle?"

Bret gripped the handle of the sword at his waist and grinned. "Something a little less obvious, I would think," he said. "We should be able to outsmart them. They don't look too bright."

"I've never seen a tormentor that was," Yolette said.

"All brawn and no brains," Anora offered.

"We have to get close to them without putting them on their guard," Bret said. "We'll act like we're drunk, lost and looking for the great hall. If they're as stupid as I think they are we should be able to get close enough to eliminate them before they know what's happening."

* * * * *

Below, in the great hall, the ruler of the realm sat savoring the carnage of the struggle being played out before him. With an evil leer, he turned to Torak.

"This year brings a particularly formidable group," he mused. "Their powers are impressive. The winner of the preliminaries should be decided soon." He grinned. "I'm anxious to see how the victor will fare against you in the final battle."

Torak smiled. "I'll not disappoint you, master," he said with confidence.

"We shall see." The master settled back in his throne. "We shall see," he repeated.

* * * * *

Staggering drunkenly, their eyes straight ahead, Bret and the women approached the doorway. As they drew near they looked at the guards, a surprised expression on their faces, as though, in their drunken state, noticing them for the first time.

"Can you help us?" Bret slurred. "We seem to be lost. Could you direct us to the great hall?"

The guards glared at Bret; then turned their attention to the women. "It's that way," the one with the javelin said, pointing the weapon in the direction the four had just come. "Now be gone. This part of the castle is for the master alone."

"Sorry to intrude," Nelda said as she moved closer to the guard, nudged the lance aside with the back of her hand, and pressed her breast to his chest. He grinned and slipped his free arm around her waist.

Suddenly, she clapped her hand over his mouth and plunged her dagger into his stomach. He groaned and slid to the floor. At the same instant Bret drew his sword and sank it, to the hilt, into the other guard's belly. With a sneer, Bret put his foot against the sentinel's chest and thrust him to the wall, violently jerking his sword free. Silently, the tormentor sank to the floor.

"Well, that takes care of the guards," Anora said. "But how do we get through the door? The bolt is padlocked."

Bret picked up the battle-axe from where the guard had dropped it. With his left hand he motioned for the women to stand back.

"We may not be able to get that padlock open," he said. "But the door is wood."

* * * * *

In the great hall the battle of demons raged on. After the initial clash, the victors, with the taste of their foe's blood in their mouths, had fallen back to gather their strength. Now they stood apart, glaring at each other, the fires of hell blazing in their bulging eyes. For a moment laden with ominous silence, they stood facing each other. Then the battle was renewed.

The wind rose again, screaming its awesome fury. Protective mantles of blue, crackling lightning materialized around the demons and sprang from their fingertips, hissing toward their opponents. With each flash of lightning came the roar of thunder. The walls of the castle trembled with each clap, and the battle began to take its deadly toll.

Lightning flashed and a male demon's severed arm flew through the air. Another cutting bolt split the abdomen of a female demon and her entrails burst forth like a bloody mass of agitated serpents. She screamed and fell to the floor, more enraged at defeat than the agonizing pain.

On the throne, the master of the castle sat with his eyelids drooping in ecstasy, a satisfied smirk on his lips.

Suddenly, he jerked bolt upright, his eyes wide and staring. His brow wrinkled and his eyes blazed with hatred as his lips twisted in a rancorous snarl. He turned to the man next to him.

"Torak!" he boomed.

Startled, Torak looked quizzically at his master. "How may I serve you?" he murmured meekly.

"Someone has dared to breach my sanctum. Go see to it."

Torak leapt from the dais and hurried across the great hall toward the stairway leading to his master's quarters.

* * * * *

Bret stood at the door, flailing away with the battle-axe while the women kept careful watch up and down the hallway. Finally, under the relentless onslaught, the door began to splinter. He increased his efforts and soon a passageway into the chamber was open.

* * * * *

When Bret and his companions stepped through the portal they felt the presence of a cold, pure evil hanging heavily in the atmosphere like a damp, moldy pall.

The room was dark and somber. Choking dust hung in the air, the torchlight flowing through the doorway giving it the appearance of a chilling fog. At the far end of the room stood a giant fireplace. Its massive stone mantle was supported, on either side, by carved busts of horned devils atop fluted columns, their faces set in expressions of unbearable agony. In the grate a fire burned. There was a table against one wall, strewn with books, their covers worn and moldy with age. In the center of this litter, a rack made of human bones held a large open book. The flickering black candles on either side cast eerie shadows across its pages. Next to the book lay a dagger, its blade as jet-black as the handle.

Bret walked to the ancient tome and ran the palm of his hand across its pages. Slowly he withdrew his hand and pressed his thumb against the tip of his fingers.

"It feels oily," he said. "I would think the pages of a book as old as that would be dry and brittle."

Yolette walked to Bret's side and raked the tips of her fingers across the pages.

"This is not a common grimoire," she said. "The pages are made of human skin and the symbols are drawn in blood." She examined the book closer. "It may be the one known as The Key of Solomon," she said. "If so, it contains spells to summon both angels and devils. According to legend, it was compiled by King Solomon himself, but lost along with the Ark of the Covenant."

"Well, it's about to be lost again," Bret said. "This time for good."

Yolette picked up the dagger lying next to the book and held it to the light of the candle.

"The athame of Asmodeus," she said with a shudder.

"Who?" Nelda asked.

"Asmodeus, the chief demon of Satan himself."

"How do you know that's his dagger?" Anora asked.

"All in the sisterhood of Wicca have heard of it," Yolette said. She held up the dagger and turned it slowly, the light glinting off its blade. "Look at it," she said. "There could be no other like it. Black as a raven's wing from pommel to tip. Wrought in a single piece from iron of a fallen meteor. Tempered by the oil of a human body by plunging it, red hot from the forge, into the breast of a lowly slave." Yolette dropped the dagger to the table in disgust. "Fitting it should be destroyed along with the grimoire," she said.

Suddenly, a harsh voice filled the room. "Damn you, you prying interlopers!" it boomed. "You'll all suffer eternal agony for this affront!"

Bret and his companions turned to see Torak standing in the doorway, his face red with rage. Before they could react he bounded into the room, his gnarled hand thrust out before him. A bolt of blue lightning shot from his fingertips, streaked across the room, and struck Anora in the breast. There was a soft hissing sound as she was thrown backward across the room.

Instinctively, Bret drew his sword and Nelda pulled her dagger form her belt. Yolette held her talisman between her thumb and forefinger and spoke in a calm, measure tone.

"By the power of Wicca," she commanded, "and the sisterhood of white witches, deliver us."

A beam of pure whiter light sprang from the iron talisman and streaked toward the advancing Torak. He snarled and thrust out his right palm deflecting the ray. With a sneer of contempt, he continued his advance. Then, with a violent push of his hand, he reversed the flow of energy, returning it to its source. Yolette let out a sharp yelp and released the charm, now burning hot to her touch.

"You pathetic novice," Torak smirked at her. "Your puny magic is no match for mine. Maybe with the accumulated knowledge of several more centuries you might have stood a chance. But that's something you will never know. Because today you and your foolish companions will suffer a fate reserved for only the lowest of crimes against the master."

While Torak's attention was on Yolette Bret sprang at him, sinking his sword deep into the warlock's side. The force of Bret's lunge carried the blade though the stomach to protrude from the other side. Torak did not fall, but faltered momentarily, more from surprise than pain. Then, in a fuming rage, the blade still in his belly, he grasped Bret with his left arm and yanked him to his chest. With a grunt of disdain he raked the talon-like fingernails of his right hand across Bret's forehead. Then he applied a torturing bearhug, lifting Bret off the floor and spinning him around.

With Torak's back to her, Yolette grabbed the athame from the table and lunged forward. In one quick movement, she grabbed a hank of hair and sliced it off with the dagger. Before the powerful warlock could react, Yolette rushed to the fireplace and threw the hair into the fire. The tress exploded in flames and acrid smoke, belching a pungent odor into the room.

The ritual had an immediate effect on Torak. He dropped Bret and turned to glare at Yolette. Then sheer terror spread across his face and he fell to his knees. His mouth gaped open emitting a soft, rasping groan. His eyes widened in horror and the groan turned to a screeching wailing like legions of tortured souls crying out in agony. Then he pitched forward, his body bursting into flames. In seconds it was reduced to a pile of gray ashes.

Bret rushed to where Anora lay. He knelt and cradled her in his arms. Her eyes fluttered, then slowly opened.

"Destroy the book," she said haltingly, her voice nearly inaudible. "Hurry, before more demons come to prevent it." Her eyes closed and she fell limp in Bret's arms. Tenderly, he lay her on the floor and slowly rose to his feet.

"Quickly," Yolette said, tugging at his arm. "We must do as she said and burn the book before it's too late. Cutting a demon's hair and burning it saps their strength, causing Satan to abandon them. Without his evil power to sustain them they perish. But destroying Asmodeus' servant only postponed the inevitable. By now he knows what we've done. He'll send a host of avenging devils against us."

Bret ran to the table and grabbed the grimoire off its rack. As he turned toward the fireplace it began to pulsate, issuing a shrill screech. The piercing noise echoed off the walls and stabbed at his eardrums.

Fighting back the excruciating pain, Bret doggedly crossed the room and heaved the book of shadows into the burning hearth. Momentarily, it lay there, the flames licking around it. Then, it began to smolder. Finally, as the piercing screams rose to a deafening pitch, it burst into a column of fire, snaking its way up the flue with a rumbling roar.

* * * * *

Downstairs, Asmodeus lurched backward in his throne as though slammed in the chest by an invisible fist. From deep beneath the floor a rumbling began. It grew louder till it overpowered even the ominous rumble of thunder. Then, with a grinding, ripping noise, the earth heaved and split. Searing flames roared up from the newly opened pit in the center of the room and spread across the floor like an exploding blast furnace.

In a panic, the witches and warlocks fled the scorching flames, crushing against the walls of the great chamber. Many were overtaken by the spreading inferno. Screaming in a single unearthly chorus, their bodies were engulfed in the holocaust.

The castle shook to its foundations and huge blocks of stone rained down on the unearthly gathering. The witches and warlocks who had escaped the fire were now being crushed by falling debris. Their shrill screams rent the air, carrying across the lake of fire into the surrounding land.

The demons hovering above the scene suddenly quit the fight and leaped toward the gaping hole in the ceiling left by the falling rocks. Concerned only with escaping Satan's wrath, they soared upward toward the black, starless sky only to collide with an invisible barrier blanketing the hall. As they slammed into the demonic shield of force they were consumed in a fiery blast.

* * * * *

Outside, in the lake of fire, the burning circle leaped higher, turning the somber gray night sky to a dull red. Then the circle began to contract, moving ever closer to the island in the center of the lake and the castle atop the summit.

Soon the flames reached the island shore. The black water turned to the color of molten lead as it churned and frothed; sending geysers of steam shooting skyward. The swirling, roaring column of flames leaped ashore and began burning toward the castle. Then, amid the wailing of the damned trapped in the fortress of evil, the island began to slowly sink, returning to the hellfire that spawned it.

* * * * *

As the castle heaved and buckled Bret was thrown to the floor. Blood from the gash on his forehead was now running into his eyes, blurring his vision. He could barely make out the figures of Nelda and Yolette kneeling near him. Through the bedlam of noise and destruction he couldn't hear what they were saying, but understood as they mouthed the words, Thank you. He smiled his acknowledgement and a sickening feeling of intense loneliness washed over him.

The scene shimmered with a ghostly light. Then, slowly it began to spin as though trapped in a giant eddy, relentlessly sucking it down into a cold, black vortex.

With the rumbling and crashing of the doomed castle and the mournful wails of the damned ringing in his ears, Bret was sucked into the churning whirlpool.

CHAPTER 21

The voice sounded far away, muffled and indistinct. Bret tried to ignore it. He was content to drift in the black void that enveloped him. He felt comfortable and strangely at peace. But the feeling was quickly eroding with the encroachment of the voice, now growing more distinct and demanding. Gradually, the black, restful void turned to a swirling gray as the voice persisted, dragging him into reality. Then he was aware of the hand on his shoulder, shaking him gently.

"Hey, mon," the voice said. "You all right?"

Slowly Bret opened his eyes. His vision was blurred and distorted. Instinctively he wiped the blood from his eyes with his sleeve and saw Mama Daka standing over him.

"You all right, mon?" she repeated.

Bret nodded. "I think so," he said in a feeble voice.

"Well, least you not dead," she said. "But you bleeding, mon." Mama Daka took the scarf from her neck and tied it around his forehead. "You need doctor, mon. I take you to doctor friend. He fix you up."

"I don't need a doctor," Bret insisted.

"You got big cut on your head, mon. You need get stitches."

Bret put his hand to the makeshift bandage on his forehead. He winced at the touch and pulled his hand away.

"Yeah, O.K.," he murmured. "I guess I could use a few stitches." Bret struggled to his feet, but his legs gave way and he fell back on the couch. "Give me a minute," he said.

"Sure, mon." Mama Daka walked to the window and threw up the sash.

"It hot here," she said. "Too hot this time of year to keep windows all closed up."

For the first time Bret was aware of the sunlight streaming through the window. The last he remembered was sitting on the couch, watching the gathering darkness of nightfall. Then the strange, gray mist that filled the room. Now the sun was shining brightly, obviously another day. He wondered how long he had been unconscious. He looked down and saw he was sill wearing the blue wizard's robe Yolette had made for him.

"Not that I'm complaining," he said, "but why did you come here today?"

"Hey, mon, you not come to town for over three weeks. I think something happen."

"How did you know I hadn't been to town for over three weeks?"

"Hey, mon, you think Mama Daka not know what go on in New Orleans? When you first come see me I decide to keep my eye on you. When you not be around I come see why. Your car outside but you not answer the door. Front door open so I come in, look for you."

"Thanks for being concerned about me."

Mama Daka shrugged her shoulders. "You need see doctor now," she said. "You get out of crazy looking bathrobe, put on some clothes."

Bret looked down at the robe again. "O.K.," he murmured, a broad smile spreading across his face.

"I wait for you on porch," Mama Daka said as she turned to leave. At the door she halted and turned back to Bret. "I talk to houngan about you," she said.

"Who?"

"Houngan. He be voodoo priest. I tell him you rich writer from New York, pay big for see voodoo ceremony. He say for fifty dollars you can watch tonight with others."

"Others?" Bret questioned.

Mama Daka smiled. "It not real," she said. "Nobody but voodoo people see real ceremony. It bullshit for tourists. But good enough for story book writing." Again she turned to leave. "Hurry," she threw back over her shoulder. "It getting late. Doctor's office close soon. I lead way in my car. You follow."

Bret rose shakily to his feet and started from the room. His eyes fell upon the painting on the mantle. The candles he had placed on either side had burned down to blobs of melted wax. He moved closer to look at the painting for a long moment, then shook his head sadly.

Anora was no longer sitting in the blue velvet upholstered chair. She was nowhere in the picture. The vibrant pink rose in the pale amber vase on the table next to the chair had turned a deep blood-red.

Bret heaved a sigh and went to his bedroom. He walked to the washstand and looked into the mirror hanging above it. A bleary-eyed, stubble bearded image stared back at him. He reached for the pitcher in the washbasin. It was empty. Sitting the pitcher down, he ran his fingers over his beard and shook his head.

"What the hell," he said softly. "Beards are supposed to be in now."

Resolutely he walked to the bed, stripped off the robe with the front stained with his blood, and tossed it in a nearby wastebasket.

* * * * *

After dressing Bret took his suitcase from the closet and threw it on the bed. As he opened it his eyes went to the robe in the wastebasket. Smiling, he retrieved it, folded it lovingly, and placed it in the bag.

I can never tell anyone about what happened, he thought. They'll think I'm crazy. In time, when the memory begins to fade, I may even begin to think it was all a dream, brought on by the atmosphere of this house. I'll need something to remind me it really happened. Something to reassure myself I'm not crazy.

Bret smiled. "Well, girls," he said in a soft, almost inaudible voice, "that will be our little secret. And, wherever you are now, I hope it's a happy place."

* * * * *

Bret walked onto the porch, not bothering to close the door behind him. He looked around as though seeing the place for the first time. For a moment he stood gazing at the surrounding landscape. After his perilous journey into a shadowy land of constant, cruel darkness, the colors, somehow, seemed more vibrant and alive than he remembered. He smiled and took a deep breath, exhaling slowly, drinking in the friendly warmth of the morning sun.

Mama Daka stood by her car at the foot of the steps and looked questioningly at the suitcase he held. Slowly, the brightness of the day began to wane. Bret looked into the distance at the approaching storm clouds, rolling black and ominous toward the city.

"It was raining the day I drove into town," he said. "Looks like it'll be raining when I leave."

"Leave?" Mama Daka questioned.

Bret nodded. "After the doctor sews me up," he said, "I'll be heading back to New York." He looked around again. "I won't be coming back here," he announced.

"But what about houngan friend and bullshit voodoo ceremony?" she asked. "You not want to see?"

Bret started down the steps toward his car. "I have what I came for," he said, again looking at the approaching storm. He smiled and tenderly rubbed the palm of his left hand across the side of the suitcase. He was sure he could feel the warmth of the robe through the leather.

Mama Daka regarded Bret suspiciously. "You all right, mon?" she asked. "You look funny."

"I'm fine," Bret assured her. "I came to New Orleans for a story, and I found one." Tenderly he rubbed the side of the suitcase again. "Not the one I was looking for," he mused. "But one hell of a story nonetheless."

THE END

About the Author

Walter F. Edwards is a prolific writer who feels equally at home in various genre. His works include Science Fiction, Horror, Fantasy, and Rough-and-tumble Adventure, all marked by vivid imagery, fast paced story advancement, and hard-hitting action.

As a twenty-year veteran of U.S. Air Force Intelligence, he has traveled extensively in the United States as well as the Orient and Europe. Some of his best yarns are laid in China and other Far Eastern countries. He served in the U.S. Air force from 1948 to 1968, and has lived in Fredericksburg, Texas with his wife, Helen, since retirement.

Printed in the United States
153048LV00002B/285/A